give
and
take

give
and
take

ELLY SWARTZ

SQUARE
FISH

FARRAR STRAUS GIROUX

New York

SQUARE
FISH

An imprint of Macmillan Publishing Group, LLC

120 Broadway, New York, NY 10271

mackids.com

Square Fish and the Square Fish logo are trademarks of Macmillan and
are used by Farrar Straus Giroux under license from Macmillan.

Our books may be purchased in bulk for promotional, educational, or business
use. Please contact your local bookseller or the Macmillan Corporate and
Premium Sales Department at (800) 221-7945 ext. 5442 or by email at
MacmillanSpecialMarkets@macmillan.com.

Library of Congress Cataloging-in-Publication Data
Names: Swartz, Elly D., author.
Title: Give and take / Elly Swartz.
Description: New York : Farrar Straus Giroux, 2019. |
Summary: When eleven-year-old Maggie's parents become temporary foster
parents for a new baby, her tendency to hoard spirals out of control.
Identifiers: LCCN 2018036025 | ISBN 978-1-250-61889-4 (paperback) |
ISBN 978-0-374-30820-9 (ebook)
Subjects: | CYAC: Family life—Fiction. | Hoarders—Fiction. | Foster home
care—Fiction. | Babies—Fiction. | Skeet shooting—Fiction.
Classification: LCC PZ7.1.S926 Giv 2019 | DDC [Fic]—dc23
LC record available at https://lccn.loc.gov/2018036025

Originally published in the United States by Farrar Straus Giroux
First Square Fish edition, 2020
Book designed by Cassie Gonzales
Square Fish logo designed by Filomena Tuosto

1   3   5   7   9   10   8   6   4   2

To my dad, whose light always shines so bright.
Love you huge.

1

Baby Girl

Baby Girl is the name written on her birth certificate, but I think that's a bit sad. Mom calls her Isabelle. That feels way too formal for a silky-soft, chubby day-old baby who smells like powder. So I name her Izzie.

I know I'm not supposed to get attached. To the baby or her name. Both are temporary. That's what Rita said. She's the woman with the rainbow-striped sweater who owns Caring Adoptions. She said this little one is with us for only a speck of time. Then she'll go to her forever family. Who will give her a forever name.

But truth is, I got attached the second I saw this bundle of sweetness. I mean, only a zombie or my big brother, Dillon, wouldn't fall in love with this tiny human with long, slender fingers that wrap around my thumb. But I'm not the only one attached.

Last night, my little brother, Charlie, said, "I love my new baby sister," as he hopped onto my lap to read *Where the Wild Things Are.*

"You know she's not your sister for keeps," I reminded him.

And myself.

"But maybe if I'm really good, she'll stay," he said, "and I'll get to be somebody's big brother."

I hugged Charlie. "It doesn't work that way, Bear."

Sadness stretched across his freckled face.

I repeated what Rita had told us—that Izzie isn't our sister for keeps. She's our sister for a smidgen. Rita said it had to do with the birth parents needing that time to make a plan. A really good plan. To decide if adoption is right for them. And, if it is, to find a loving home with a loving family. So in two days, two weeks, or a month, we'll need to return our little bundle to Rita and the agency.

Like a library book.

But I don't want to tell Charlie that.

Because to me, she feels like my baby sister.

Even if it's for just a few days.

2

The Green Jell-O Declaration

I'm not really supposed to call her *my* sister. That was another thing Rita told me in our meeting after the green Jell-O declaration.

It was Try-This Tuesday family dinner. No one had guessed the experimental ingredient in our maybe-meat lasagna. Not Gramps, Dad, Dillon, Charlie, or me. Green Jell-O with yellow and red fruit chunks was for dessert. Mom was superproud of it. I've never really been a fan of desserts that jiggle and contain no chocolate. But Mom told me it was a special one that Nana used to make when Mom was a little girl, so I took a bite. Then Mom stood up and said, "Dad and I have an announcement."

Dillon and I looked at each other. The last *big* announcement was that they'd bought new salt and pepper shakers shaped like our dog Batman. I'm not sure that qualified as announcement-worthy. But then Mom said, "We've decided to take in a newborn baby awaiting adoption."

Mom smiled like she was full of happiness, so I told my parents that I thought it was a good idea. Dillon wanted to know if this meant he couldn't try out for the travel basketball team, and Charlie danced around the kitchen, chanting, "I'm going to be a big brother!"

The next day, after my parents reassured Dillon that he could still try out and told Charlie that our fostering was short-term, we took a family field trip to Caring Adoptions. Mom said Rita had to be certain we'd be good temporaries.

I wasn't sure what that meant until Izzie arrived with tiny fingers and steel-blue eyes and the smell of powder. Now I know that taking care of little ones for a speck of time is an important job. Maybe the most important.

Caring Adoptions was bright, and the bells on the

office door chimed when we entered. Rita greeted us, and said that she'd talk to Dillon first, me second, then Charlie with Mom and Dad. While Dillon met with her, Charlie sat on the green carpet, playing with a floppy teddy bear. Mom and Dad held hands at the too-small table. Mom looked happier than I'd seen her in a while. Her face was soft and warm. And less sad. After Nana died a year ago from some infection that crept into her lung, Mom had a great big hole in her heart. I know because I had one, too. Mom said I shouldn't worry. She just needed time. To heal.

But then last month, Mom put on her Women-in-Charge T-shirt and went to a conference for women-run small businesses. Mom joined the group when she started The Application Adviser, to helps kids applying to college. At the morning workshop on networking strategies, she met Rita and learned that a newborn was coming who needed a home. A loving home. For a short time.

After Mom's big announcement, I realized that maybe Mom didn't really need time. Maybe she just needed a new little human to love.

I sank into the big, fluffy blue couch in the waiting room and wondered if it was that way on purpose. To make visitors like me feel safe. And tucked-in. Then I looked around and realized I was surrounded by hundreds of cards with pictures of smiling babies and happy parents, and words like *wonder*, *peace*, *miracle*, and *joy*.

When Dillon came out of Rita's office, it was my turn to go in.

Rita was wearing a sweater with all the colors of the rainbow. I liked the orange stripe best. It reminded me of Pumpkin Pie, my favorite colored pencil. The sign above Rita's desk said:

A NEW BABY IS THE BEGINNING OF ALL THINGS—WONDER, HOPE, A DREAM OF POSSIBILITIES.—EDA LESHAN

"Hi, Maggie. Thanks for coming." Rita offered me a piece of butterscotch candy from the bowl on her desk. The candy reminded me of Nana. Butterscotch was her favorite. I wondered if that's something she remembers in heaven.

We talked for a while about seventh grade, apple picking at Billow's Orchard, and how chocolate cake with chocolate icing and chocolate chips might be the best dessert ever. Then she asked, "How do you feel about being a foster sister?"

"Sounds good. I mean, I like being a sister, so I think I'll like this, too. Plus, babies are supercute, and Mom and Dad said these babies really need us."

"That's true. These babies do need lots of love. This is an important job, Maggie. A special kind of fostering. It's for a few days, a week, or a handful of weeks at most, until the babies can go to their forever families."

I twirled the candy around my mouth with my tongue. "Can I ask you something?"

"Sure. Anything." Rita popped one of the butterscotch candies into her mouth.

"If these little ones are going to be adopted, why do they need us? I mean, why don't they just go right to their forever families?"

"In Massachusetts, birth parents can't sign papers allowing an adoption until four days after birth."

"Why?"

"It gives the birth parents time to select their baby's forever family and to make sure adoption is the best decision for them and the baby. That's where I come in. I help them find a loving short-term foster family that can take care of their baby while they're figuring these things out."

"Like us."

"Yes, like all of you," Rita said. "But remember, Maggie, *you're* not the baby's forever sister." She smiled. "Your family's job is to help this little one have a wonderful start to life. And not to get too attached."

Turns out I'm not so good at that last part.

3

Eagle Eyes

I wake extra early when I hear Izzie stir on her first morning as a sort-of member of the Hunt family. I hop out of bed, grab Bud the Bear, slide into my fuzzy slippers, and twirl my ruby-red hair into the clip Charlie bedazzled with rhinestones for my twelfth birthday. When I walk into Izzie's room, her cry doesn't sound like sadness. It sounds like, *Hey, anyone awake?*

"I am," I say as I gently cradle her tiny body against my chest. I spin around so she can see the black-and-white elephant pictures that Mom hung above the white straw bassinet that Dad rolled into the office yesterday. Mom says the color contrast is good for a baby's eyes and brain. I'm not sure if that's true, but I stand there for a minute just in case. Then I tackle the whole diaper thing. Mom taught me how to wipe, tuck, and fold when Charlie was born. Dad says I'm a natural. I think he says that because he hates changing dirty diapers.

When I'm done, I sing "Lullaby Blue" to a clean and happy Izzie, in the rocking chair that used to be Nana's. Izzie stares at me with her big blue eyes. Batman licks her toes and then sinks his gigantic body next to us. Four years ago, Dad showed up with a Labrador retriever puppy. A sweet black ball of fur that Mom called a disaster. Until she fell in love with him. Now she calls Batman family.

I pick up Bud the Bear. "Okay, Little Bean. When I was born, Dillon gave me Bud. Now I'm giving him to you. To borrow. He's soft and will watch over you. I promise. He's watched over me for the last twelve years." I set Bud the Bear on the wooden table next to the bassinet.

"I'll take her now," Mom says from the doorway in her beige robe, tired dripping from her eyes. Turns out Izzie was up most of the night.

"Dad's making breakfast, and then you guys have to get to practice. It's Saturday."

I kiss my baby sister's soft cheek and hand her to my mother.

"You know, you have a beautiful voice," Mom says. I'd forgotten that part. The part where there's now a baby monitor in the room so she and Dad can supervise the care of our tiny human. And listen to me sing.

I inhale a plate of the best banana pancakes ever and sneak Batman a piece of I-love-my-dog bacon.

An hour later, I'm looking down the barrel of my trap shotgun. I line up the beads the way Dad showed me, one stacked on top of the other. He calls it "the snowman." A trick he taught me when I first started trap. I'd been tagging along with him for years to his sportsmen's club, Fish, Fur, and Fly. Everyone knew him there. He'd been coming since before he met Mom. Eventually, when I turned ten and was old enough to shoot on the junior squad, he showed me the snowman.

My mind turns to Izzie. Rita had said she'll likely be with us for only a few days or a week. And then all that sweetness will be gone. Except for that thing I saved. I took it this morning after pancakes. Dad was in the kitchen and Mom was downstairs giving Izzie her bottle. They don't know. No one knows.

It's my secret.

A little something. To remember.

So my memories don't disappear.

So I don't forget Izzie.

Like Nana forgot me.

I focus my eyeballs on the top of the trap house, where I imagine the bright-orange clay pigeon will spring from. I yell, "Pull!" as the world stops breathing. Then I see it. Feel it. Hit it. The pumpkin-colored disc shatters into a million pieces of confetti in the air. I watch the bright-orange rain while the smell of sulfur dances under my nose.

I love this moment.

Ava gives me a way-to-go nod. Sam doesn't move. Her eyes are laser-focused, and wisps of her midnight-black hair fly out from under her Red Sox cap. She stares into the sky, waiting for her turn. Ava's next, then Sam, Gracie, and Belle. I spy Gracie's purple socks peeking out from her jeans. Ever since she scored 23/25 while wearing them, she's worn them to every single practice and shoot. After the first fifteen rounds, I'm leading, Ava's in second, Sam's in last place. Twice she's grazed the disc. But no shatter, no rain, no confetti. So no points. I glance over and give her a don't-worry-you've-got-this smile, but she turns away.

"Bring it in," Coach calls out, stroking his black-and-gray beard. "Pizza's here!"

The five of us huddle around the wooden picnic table next to the range. Gracie tries to tuck her short blond hair behind her ears, forgetting she just cut off ten inches to donate to Locks of Love. We're the first-ever all-girl squad on Fish, Fur, and Fly's Eagle Eyes team. I joined Eagle Eyes in fifth grade, as one of the juniors. Then in sixth grade, I dragged in a few of my friends, who rallied a few of their friends. By the time we were done, we were an all-girl squad in a mostly boy sport. Mom got us T-shirts that read GIRL POWER across the front.

Coach walks over, thanks the delivery guy, and sets the pizza down on the picnic table. He's sort of a big deal around here. He was the top trapshooter for the club five years in a row. The best part most days is that he's also my dad.

"Next week, I'm adding an extra practice on Wednesday, and then it'll be the usual on Saturday," Dad says. "Be sure to bring your lucky socks, coins, shirts—whatever you need to work the magic."

"Trap's not about superstition," Sam says as she pulls the pepperoni off a slice lying in the box and adds it to her own. "It's about practice and skill."

Gracie slides her pant legs over her purple socks.

"Oh, and one more thing," Dad says. "After those practices, there are going to be some changes to the squad."

I freeze. *What? He didn't say anything about changes at breakfast. Or ever.*

"We're putting together the strongest squad from all the shooters at Fish, Fur, and Fly."

The cheese sticks in my throat. My brain scans the five squads Dad could choose from.

"What does that mean?" Gracie asks.

"That Mason Lloyd will be joining our squad," Ava says.

"And one of us will be leaving," I say.

4

A Whole Heap

Ava stands up, elbows pointy, hands on her hips. "We don't need a boy on our squad to make it better." Her lips tighten. The way they do when her four older brothers tell her she's too young, too girl, too everything to play with them. Gracie nods while taking the pepperoni off her pizza and handing it to Sam.

Dad grabs another slice. "I never said we *needed* a boy on our squad to make it better. I also never said it was Mason Lloyd who will be joining us. All I said was that a change was coming."

"Look, as long as this new person can help our squad win the state shoot, I think it's a good move,"

Sam says, the sun making her dark eyes look black as night.

"You know, Coach," Ava says, "Mason Lloyd may be a good shooter, but he burped the entire alphabet for the middle school talent show."

I look over at Dad.

Don't do this. Don't break up our squad.

"I hear what you're all saying, but at this point, I'm not discussing who the new squad member might be. For now, let's just focus on finishing this pizza."

Then I see it in a puddle under the table. All by itself. I stop thinking about someone leaving our squad. Stop listening to Ava talk about how Dad's breaking up the Original Five and put my hand on the ground and wait. After a few minutes, it gingerly climbs in, tickling my palm with its tiny claws.

"I have to get this little guy back to his family."

Everyone turns my way. I open my palm, and sitting in the middle is a turtle with a bright-orange belly and a heart-shaped marking on his brown shell.

Dad nods. This isn't the first stray animal I've

helped. A few years ago, I brought home Ginger, a bird with a broken wing. I couldn't just leave her hopping in circles. So Mom and I took her to Dr. Yang, the veterinarian who smells like spearmint, and we cared for her until she was ready to fly home. Before that it was Fred the frog.

Ava and I run across the field and down the hill, to the edge of Baker's Pond. The mud seeps into the side of my boot, where Batman chewed a nickel-size hole last week after eating Dillon's Nerf basketball.

"Okay, little guy," I say as I gently open my hand.

The turtle walks across my fingers and onto a rock in the water on the side of the range.

Back to his family.

The windows are down on the drive home from trap. It's not helping. Dad's car still smells like leftover pepperoni pizza. I turn to him as he slows to a stop at the corner of Dudley and Baron Drive. "How can you break up our squad?"

"I'm not breaking up anything. Everyone on the

squad will remain a part of the larger Eagle Eyes team."

"Just not a member of *our* five-person, all-girl squad," I say. "I'm the squad leader. I should have a say."

He shakes his head. "You lead this squad. That's your job. I create the squads. That's my job. Besides, I'm just shuffling people around the different squads to make each one the strongest it can be."

"Shuffling people around *and* breaking up the squad both end with our all-girl trap squad not being an all-girl trap squad anymore." I stick my hand out the window, let the air flow through my fingers, and stop listening to my dad's speech on team dynamics and coaching and blah-blah-blah. Nothing he says is going to change that, come the end of next week, one of the Original Five will be gone, and with it, all our girl power.

When we get home, I hop out of the car and carry my trap bag with my shotgun to the gun safe in the basement. Dad follows me. Only he and Mom have the combination. A two-parent nonnegotiable rule. Dad puts the gun in the safe and locks it, and

I head back to Dillon, who's playing basketball in the driveway. He's wearing Dad's old #33 Larry Bird jersey, and it almost fits him.

"Want to shoot around?" he asks, swishing a foul shot with the basketball Dad got him after Dillon confessed he had no interest in trapshooting.

I nod.

Dillon passes me the ball, and I knock in a left-handed layup. He's the one who taught me how to shoot lefty. "Is Izzie home?" I ask.

"Nope. Mom took her somewhere."

I let the rebound fall. My breath catches in the place that holds my worries.

"Not to her new family?" *It's too soon.*

He shrugs and chases the rebound.

I'm not ready.

"Dillon, where did they go?" My voice coated with desperation. *I need to know.*

"No idea." He sinks a three-pointer from the top of the driveway.

My body tightens. I think back. *Did Mom leave a note or text me about saying good-bye?* I search my brain but find only blank space.

"Oh, wait. I think she went to get more baby stuff. I guess you need a lot of diapers and formula when all you do is eat and poop." Dillon hits another three. "Don't see why it matters, anyway. If she's not leaving today, it'll be soon."

He may be right, but it still matters.

To me.

A whole heap.

5

The Kind of Thing
Big Sisters Do

I lose to Dillon. It's sort of inevitable. He's on the high school varsity team. As a freshman. But the last time we played, I came closer to winning. He beat me with a backward eyes-closed shot from the crack on the far-right side of the driveway. Okay, so maybe I wasn't that close, but closer.

While Mom's out doing baby errands, I sneak into Izzie's room. It smells like talcum. And love. Before this, I didn't even know that love had a smell.

I peek into the white straw bassinet. It's hard to believe anything other than Charlie's stuffed T. rex fits in here.

Last night, Mom laid Izzie in the bassinet, and then she and I waited until Izzie fell asleep. It was her first night with our family, and neither of us wanted to leave her. We sat on the gray-and-cream-swirl carpet listening to the sound of Izzie's sweet breath. Mom pulled a photo off the shelf. It was a picture of Charlie as a baby resting on my six-year-old lap. His tar-black sprig of hair, and beautiful round eyes looking into my big sister face. I was in first grade, learning about the life cycle of a frog when Charlie was born. Mom said I wanted to know if Charlie was hatched.

We sat like that for a while last night. It reminded me of that time with Nana. It was a little over a year ago, a few months before she died. I'd just come home from trap practice. Nana was in the kitchen with Mom. The way she had been a hundred times before. She was wearing the soft navy sweater I'd helped her pick out and drinking iced coffee with lots of milk. She looked up at me.

"Hi, Nana," I said.

She said nothing.

And that's when I felt it. She didn't know *me*. She saw a girl with long, wild red hair and green eyes. A girl with a peace sign on her shirt. But that girl wasn't the granddaughter she'd loved forever.

That girl was just a girl.

Any girl.

I ran from the kitchen into this room. Batman was here. He snuggled into my body as I cried. I'd been forgotten. By someone who'd loved me my whole life.

Mom found me after Nana went home, and we sat together on the swirly carpet, sadness filling the space between us. That day, my heart shattered into a million tiny pieces.

My nana had forgotten.

All of me.

I look around the room now and am happy it's flooded with the smell of powder and sweetness. Tiny human love. And wipes, binkies, and board books. Mom says research shows that babies love the sound of your voice when they're being read to. Mom's into research and studies, and things that make sense. I grab *Pat the Bunny*.

I run my hands across the pages. The tuft of the bunny's tail feels soft against my palm.

I wonder if Izzie will remember me reading this to her.

Giving her a bottle.

Being her sister.

It's been twenty-four hours.

I head to my room, turn on my speakers, and let the music of "I Found You" by Alabama Shakes fall around me. I slide one of the brown cardboard boxes out from under my bed. I took it from the recycle bin. It was the one that Batman came in. Not the actual black Lab who eats my shoes and steals my socks, but the stuffed animal version I got for Hanukkah last year. The other boxes in my closet were too full to add even one more thing after I saved the green bath mat from the garbage. Mom had thrown it away, like she didn't care about all those times my toes had touched the fuzzy kiwi-colored mat.

I lift the lid and see the gecko necklace from Nana. She gave it to me when I was nine for no special reason. That's what she said. It was a just-because-I-love-you present. It's blue with a speck of gold, and

I wore it every day until the day she forgot me. Then I took it off and put it in one of my boxes. Where I could never lose it. Or forget it.

When Nana died last year, I added a tassel from her favorite pomegranate-red scarf. And since then, I've added five gum wrappers; three bendy straws; sticks from a hike up Ridge Mountain, Wade's Pond, and a walk with Charlie; a yellow plastic fork; half a red, white, and blue plate with a picture of fireworks on it; and a butterscotch candy wrapper. I've also filled the seven boxes in the closet, the three others under my bed, and most of my school locker.

Today, I drop in one teeny-tiny yellow sock.

A little piece of Izzie.

For me.

To keep.

"What are you doing?" It's Charlie.

"Um, just looking for something," I say, quickly closing my box and shoving it back under my bed. Hidden. From everyone.

"Did you know the heart of a shrimp is in its head?"

I stare at my baby brother, wondering how his little six-year-old brain can hold so much random stuff.

"I didn't," I say.

"Also, last week I found Shira's reading journal *and* the class watering can. My teacher says I'm the world's best finder. I can help. What are we looking for?"

"Got it!" I say, holding nothing.

"Got what?"

"Oh, I realized what I was looking for isn't even really lost. I forgot that I already put it in my backpack."

"That was kind of what happened with the watering can. Turns out, Jeremiah left it outside by the baby ficus tree we planted last year for Principal James on Principals' Day." He hops onto the end of my bed. "What stinks?"

"Nothing," I say.

"It's kind of like minty throw-up," he says, his nose all scrunched up.

I remember when my baby brother smelled like powder. He was two months old, and Mom and I brought him into Ms. Sherman's first-grade class for circle time sharing. That same day, my friend Juan brought in his pet lizard named Slither. I don't have circle time in seventh grade, but if I did, I'd ask Mom to bring Izzie.

Charlie hands me a card. It's the shape of a star, and it's covered in rainbow-colored pom-poms. "I made this for Izzie." Sweetness splashed all over his face.

"It's beautiful, Bear. I know she'll love it."

"I'm going to make her a card every day. That's the kind of thing a big brother does."

My heart tears a bit. "Remember what we talked about last night?"

He gives me the smallest of nods. "I know. She's not my sister for keeps."

I reach over and hug my little brother.

Because that's the kind of thing big sisters do.

6

A Handful of Dandelions and a Few Fat Worms

After school on Wednesday, I head to trap for the extra practice Dad added so our squad will have the six practices needed to qualify for the state tournament. I don't care that it's hot and sticky and my Girl Power shirt clings to my back, because today everyone is here. Today, we're still the Original Five. Still an all-girl trap squad—me, Ava, Belle, Gracie, and Sam.

The air's thick, and beads of sweat trickle down my neck as I position my feet and lean forward, careful not to lose my balance. I raise my shotgun and see the orange disc fly out of the trap house. My excitement surges from that place that knows the disc's path. I squeeze the trigger and shoot. As pieces of tangerine fill the sky, happiness zips up from my boots.

I shoot a 20/25. A good day. I'm up to fifteen push-ups and almost eight pull-ups. Dad says the stronger I am, the better I'll shoot. Maybe he's right.

As we wrap up practice and head to our squad meeting at the picnic table, Ava whispers, "Did you talk your dad out of mixing up the squad?" She's wearing her Girl Power shirt, too.

"Tried, but no luck." I pop a strawberry lollipop in my mouth.

"We can't be an *almost*-all-girl squad. It's not the same," she says, pointing to her T-shirt.

Sam grabs an apple-green lollipop from the big bowl on the picnic table. "Look, if Mason or whoever joins our squad and makes it better, then maybe it's not a bad idea. I mean, I'm all for girl power and sisterhood, but I want to win."

I look down and see a turtle. I know it's my friend from the other day when I spy the heart-shaped marking on his shell.

I scoop him up. He's about the size of my phone.

This time, I tuck him and the rock he's sitting on into my open vest pocket. With a handful of dande-lions.

Quietly.

Slowly.

Carefully.

So when I leave trap and Dad parks his truck in the driveway of our brick home with the bright-blue door—the one Mom painted so people could easily find our house—I don't talk about practice or the still-all-girl squad or the new color of our front door. Instead, I go straight to the garage. My turtle friend needs a forever home.

I find a big plastic tub, empty Dad's jumper cables, wrenches, and mound of extension cords onto the neighboring shelf, and scrub off the dirt and dust that's caked onto the sides. When it stops smelling like Dad stuff, I fill it with water and head to the backyard to get some of the rocks that Batman's dug up.

Then I bring the tub into my room. Push aside my beanbag chair with the plaid duct-tape over the hole, my dirty clothes, and old sketch pad, to make room for the new home. Carefully, I remove the little guy from my pocket and hold him in my hands. His orange belly is so bright and beautiful. I place my hard-shelled buddy into the tub, take out my phone, and do a quick search.

Turns out he's an eastern painted turtle. I hop online to see what else this little guy needs. I search a bunch of caring-for-your-pet-turtle sites.

"What should I call you?"

His back legs stretch, but his head stays tucked in his shell.

"What about Bert?" That was the name of my favorite class pet–a beautiful garter snake who lived in Mr. O's second-grade room and loved juicy slugs.

Slowly, I see the tip of my turtle's nose untuck, then his head.

"Welcome home, Bert."

I hand him a piece of romaine lettuce I swiped from the refrigerator. "So happy I don't have to get permission from Rita to keep you. She doesn't have to say I'll be a loving family who can do this super-important job. Because I already know."

I sneak into Dillon's room and borrow his heat

lamp. Last year, he used it for some school science experiment to see if beans grow faster with artificial heat or sunlight. Neither worked, because Batman ate all the beans. I clip the heat lamp to the side of the tub, careful it doesn't touch the plastic, and turn it on. I feel the warmth ooze out.

Next, food. Turns out, Bert's an omnivore. I give him another piece of romaine, then run back outside and gather a handful of dandelions and a few fat worms. I check the websites one more time to be sure I haven't missed anything. When everything's in place, I peek over the tub. "Okay, buddy. You're home now."

I promise him that I'll be his family.

For keeps.

7

The Napping Room

I use a little baby shampoo to wash off any leftover
pond grime, then watch Bert swim in his new home
while I practice my speech. Over and over and over
again. When Bert stops swimming to bask on a
rock under the warmth of the heat lamp, I take it as
a sign that I'm ready. And persuasive. I scoop him
up, inhale all the courage floating in the air around
me, and walk downstairs.

"Um, hello?" I say.

Dad rolls over like he wasn't just sound asleep on
the brown leather couch under the blue afghan Nana
crocheted before she forgot how. The one that feels

like the best hug ever. "Hi," he says, ignoring my snoring mom and drooling dog who are also asleep on the couch.

"Why is everyone sleeping?" I look around the Napping Room.

"Isabelle," Dad says. "She was up a lot last night. So neither of us got much sleep. Thought I'd just lie down for a little. What's up?"

I pause and scour my brain for what I was going to say, but can't remember my rehearsed speech. So I just hold out my hard-shelled friend. "Meet Bert. I made him a home in my room." I quickly add, "I promise I'll take good care of him and he'll be no extra work for you."

Mom chooses this moment to stifle her snores and open her eyes. "Maggie, sweetheart, you can't save everything," she says.

"But I can try." I hold Bert close to my chest. He smells like baby shampoo. And worms.

Before Mom or Dad can respond, Charlie comes in, spies Bert, and says, "Did you know turtles fart?"

We all laugh.

Then Mom puts her serious face back on. "I know he's cute. And you want to give him a good home. I'm just not sure this is the right time."

"Mom, please," I say, then look over at my dad. "Bert's an eastern painted turtle, just like Bob Dylan." That was Dad's turtle when he was a kid. I've seen pictures. They look like twins, minus Bert's heart-shaped splotch.

Dad smiles. Then looks at Mom. "How about Bert can stay as long as Dr. Yang checks him out and gives him the okay."

Mom turns to me. "And you wash your hands after touching him—especially before you hold Isabelle. And you clean his home."

"I promise."

"I'll call Dr. Yang's office today and see when we can bring this little guy over," Dad says.

I like Dr. Yang. She takes care of Batman and all the different animals I've found through the years. Last time I was there, she said I needed an ANIMAL RESCUER button.

"And one more thing. You need to find another

plastic tub in the garage for all Dad's stuff," Mom says.

"Wait, I didn't even tell you about the tub." I stare at my parents, wondering if they have superpowers.

"Parents know things. Even when we're sleeping." Mom smiles.

That kind of freaks me out *and* makes me happy. Not that they know stuff, but that Mom seems less sad since Izzie got here. Maybe we're all less sad.

The first worst day of my life: Forgot-Me Day. The second worst day of my life was last year at Nana's funeral. The funeral home was cold and damp, and everything was beige. Before the service, Dad and I went into a small, narrow room with a velvet curtain. I recognized the smell from biology class. Embalming fluid. Dad said I didn't have to do this part, but I told him I wanted to say goodbye. He held my hand. I held my breath. Nana wore her favorite teal sweater, and her nails were painted Dragon Red. She looked like Nana, but not really.

Truth was, she hadn't really looked like Nana since she'd forgotten me. I mean, on the outside she looked the same, but the Nana who had loved me so completely my whole life was gone. After Forgot-Me Day, over tears and iced tea with lots of honey, Mom told me and my brothers that Nana had something called dementia. A disease that makes your brain forget things. Little things. Big things. Then most things. It sounded like walking in the dark. With no flashlight or nightlight or stars.

I told Nana that I was going to miss her and confessed I was kind of mad that she'd forgotten me, but promised I'd forgive her. Just maybe not today. Then I leaned down and kissed her forehead.

8

Dried Mango and Other Stuff

I leave the nappers, put Bert in his new home, and wash my hands. Twice. I slide onto the carpeted floor of my closet and check on my boxes—the ones that Mom thinks are filled with stuff I've saved from school. She's not entirely wrong, I guess. There is the self-portrait I did in first grade and the dirt cups and lima beans I used for my sprout project in third grade. But there's also the shirt I wore in second grade when Nana and I went to The Scoop. We got root beer floats. I'd never had one. Nana said we had to fix that. So she picked me up after school and took me to The Scoop. We sat on the counter stools and she ordered us each a root beer float while I spun circles on my stool. I remember the fizz and the ice cream were so good together. The shirt hasn't fit me for years, but I could never throw that memory away. It's right next to the orange-and-white-striped bathing suit I wore when I passed the deep-water swim test in second grade. I tossed it in the box that day even though it wasn't totally dry. Then I told Mom I lost it.

I open the lid of the next box and see the Chinese takeout containers from the last time Nana and I shared Kung Pao chicken. After we finished dinner, Nana rinsed the containers and tossed them into the recycle bin. When she walked out of the kitchen to give something to Gramps, I retrieved the containers, stuffed them in my backpack, took them home, and added them to my box.

I survey to make sure everything is still where it should be. Then I close my closet door and walk down the hall to find my temporary baby sister. She's lying in the bassinet. It's been five days since the first moment I saw her, sleeping in her car seat with her mint-green onesie and sprig of brown hair. I pick her up, careful to support her head and neck. A lesson Mom and Dad gave us on how to hold this tiny person. Her skin is the softest I've ever felt.

We rock for a while until Dillon comes in.

"Heard about your new turtle and about the changes in the squad," he says, following the swirls on the carpet with his big toe. The one with no toenail. It popped off about a month ago after some kid with ginormous feet came down hard on his foot during a basketball game. Dillon's toenail turned black and then just fell off.

"Bert's cool. You'll like him. He's superfast, like you," I say.

"Who do you think will get bumped?" he asks.

My insides crumble thinking about losing one of the Original Five.

"Don't know," I say even though that's not entirely true. I worry it might be Belle. While Sam's had a few bad rounds recently, Belle's been the weakest shooter overall since she joined the squad. But I don't even want to think it, because I don't want to risk putting it into the universe. The best thing you can do if you really want something is to send it into the world. Tell the universe. But if you don't want something, you say nothing. You don't even think it.

Dillon takes three sticks of bubble gum from his pocket and stuffs them in his mouth.

Then my phone rings. In my bedroom. "Hey, will you hold Izzie so I can grab that?" I ask.

He shakes his head no while blowing a double bubble.

"Please. I'll be superquick."

He inhales the bubble before it pops. "Nope."

"Why not?" I honestly don't know how he could not want to hold her.

"This kid is part-time. Her mom gave her to us, total strangers, the same way the people who work at Nature's Food give out free samples of dried mango."

"You can't compare Izzie to dried mango. We're not strangers. We're family."

My phone stops ringing.

"Family's not something that lasts days or weeks. It's an always thing."

That's something we agree on.

"Look, I'm fine with her being here," he says. "I

just don't want to be involved. Besides, all she does is eat, poop, and sleep."

And love.

Batman walks in and licks our baby's little toes, and we both laugh.

My phone starts ringing again.

I seize the moment, hand Izzie to Dillon, and hold my breath.

Just feel her soft, buttery skin.

Look in her eyes.

And then tell me you don't totally love her.

"Fine, get your phone."

As I head down the hall, I hear Dillon talking to Izzie. "So, do you like basketball? I taught Maggie a solid left-handed layup. Wonder if you'll be a righty or lefty."

I smile.

The phone's no longer ringing when I get to my room. I look at the missed calls. They're both from Ava. I text that I'm with Izzie and will call later. I tuck my phone in my pocket and head back. Dillon quickly hands Izzie to me like he wasn't just talking to her. Like he doesn't wonder if she'll be able to do a left-handed layup.

"Do you think she'll remember us?" I ask him. I've been thinking about this a lot. Mom said we don't do this to be remembered. We do this because it's important work. Because we have love to give. But still. The thought of Izzie forgetting me—like Nana did—hurts. All the way through my bones.

"No," he says. "She's too little to remember anything. And it's not like it really matters. She'll be gone soon."

I nod.

But in my whole heart, it matters to me.

9

Spaghetti and Meatballs for Six

Dillon leaves to practice his three-point shot. I kiss a sleeping Izzie's forehead the way Nana used to kiss mine and go back to my room. This time, I grab one of the boxes from under my bed. I like the feel of the cardboard next to me. I open the lid and drop in the rock I took when I scooped up Bert at the field. It lands next to Izzie's sock. I close the lid. Tightly. My box is just for me.

To hold.

My stuff.

For keeps.

Mom calls upstairs that it's dinnertime. I leave

my room, head to the kitchen, and run smack into random fact #147.

"Do you know the longest pasta noodle ever was twelve thousand three hundred eighty-eight feet and five inches?" Charlie asks.

I look at my parents, wondering whose gene is responsible for this.

"Are you sure?" Dillon asks.

"Yep," Charlie says. "Saw it in the *Guinness World Records* book that Nana and Gramps gave me for Hanukkah last year."

No one corrects him, but the air is filled with Nana-wasn't-here-for-Hanukkah-last-year. She had died two months earlier.

I reach for Gramps's hand under the table, and he gives mine a little squeeze.

Baby Izzie stares wide-eyed at my little brother. She has no idea about Nana or the forgetting or the amount of obscure stuff Charlie has stored in his brain. Last week, he told me if I'm ever stuck in the jaws of a crocodile, all I need to do is push my thumb into its eyeball and it will let me go instantly.

A yellow knit cap sits on Izzie's tiny head. It was one of the few things that came with her. I'd walked in from school and saw her sleeping in Mom's arms. She had a tuft of acorn-brown hair, ocean-blue eyes, and the tiniest toes. So beautiful.

I looked at this teeny human who my mother was holding.

She didn't feel like a stranger.

She felt like she was exactly where she belonged.

Charlie springs up from the dinner table. "Can I hold her? Please, please, please," he asks, walking over to Baby Izzie. She's lying in a bouncy seat that's covered with blue dolphins and a big yellow sun.

I look at Mom and Dad. Then at Gramps, who's twirling his spaghetti. I wasn't going to be the one to grant permission. The last time I gave Charlie something precious to hold, he was four. I handed him my trapshooting medal for placing second in the junior club championship, and he flushed it down the toilet. Mom had to call Larry the plumber.

"Charlie, if you sit back down in your seat, I'll rest Isabelle on your lap," Mom says.

Charlie brushes the curls out of his eyes and eases himself into his chair, arms out. Mom gently places my new sister in his lap. In my head, I know she's not *my* sister, but in my heart, she's all mine. Charlie stares at Izzie and says, "I think her whole body is smaller than the ears on the rabbit with the longest ears."

"How long are his ears?" I ask, unsure if this is another *Guinness World Records* book fact.

"Thirty-one inches," Charlie says, stroking Izzie's little feet.

"Izzie *is* smaller!" Dad says, then jots something down in his little notebook. I wonder if those pages know who's being cut from our team.

He told me this book is where he saves his greatest story ideas for his podcast, *Go On, Change the World!* Dad's a radio producer for WBGT, and when he's not at the station, he's recording his podcast in the linen closet where Mom keeps all the towels. Last year he lined the walls of the closet with sound-absorbent foam and piled blankets on the floor, and when he's recording, he pops a sign on the door that says RECORDING IN PROGRESS. NO TOWELS NOW. So on those days, I shower in the morning.

"I think she likes me," Charlie squeals. "She's smiling."

"Pretty sure that's gas," Dillon says.

Charlie looks up at me with his chocolate-brown eyes.

"No way. That's a real smile," I say. "She totally loves you."

I grab my phone off the counter and snap a pic of my little brother with my new baby sister.

When I met with Rita, she said that photos are an important part of Izzie's Life Book. I didn't even know Izzie had a Life Book. But Rita said it holds the pictures and letters that we'll send with Izzie when she gets adopted by her forever family. She said these things will tell her story from the day she was born. So far, I have a photo of her in the bouncy seat. Batman with the blue toy whale he drags every-where. Dad drinking coffee from his I ♥ MY DAD mug. Mom sitting at the table in the office reading over her students' college essays. Dillon shooting hoops in Dad's Larry Bird jersey. Gramps weeding his garden. And each one of us holding her. This way, when she leaves to go to her new family, she'll take a little bit of us with her.

I get the cutest picture of Charlie hugging Baby Izzie. Then Mom gathers her up and returns her to the bouncy seat.

Back to spaghetti and meatballs for six.

"Who wants to go first?" Dad asks.

"Not me," Dillon says, sneaking a look at his phone.

Charlie's hand shoots in the air. "I do."

"All right, let's hear it."

"What made me happy today was making a card for my new baby sister." He looks at Mom. "I mean, my new baby *foster* sister. This one had pictures of an elephant and a hippopotamus. No pom-poms. Just some feathers."

Dad smiles at Mom.

"What made me sad was remembering that Izzie isn't my baby sister for keeps."

Mom nods.

"What made me mad was thinking about Emma Rose not letting me play four square at school."

"Why?" Dillon asks, dumping two more gigantic meatballs onto his plate.

"She told me it was a new kind of four square that she just made up and I didn't know the rules."

I see the sadness leak into my little brother's eyes.

"Tell her you're a fast learner. Just like you're a fast finder."

Charlie smiles. Mom whispers something in his ear and kisses his forehead to make his whole world better.

"You're up, Maggie," Dad says. We've been doing the happy, mad, sad thing every night at dinner since I was Charlie's age.

"What made me happy was rocking with Izzie, finding Bert, and shooting a 20/25 at trap. What made me sad was thinking about saying good-bye to my baby sister. What made me mad was Dad breaking up our trap family."

"I'm not breaking up the squad, Maggie. I'm just making adjustments. That's all," he says.

It's Dillon's turn, but he's texting.

There's a strict no-phone policy at the dinner table. It's a rule. A Mom Rule.

Mom opens her hand, and Dillon puts his phone in her palm. He says his happy is Pasta Wednesday. He has no sad. His mad is understood.

10

Happy Mode

Turns out we're able to get an appointment with Dr. Yang the next day after school. Mom can't make it, but Dad's free to take me and Bert. When we walk in, I spy a photograph of a giant bullfrog on the wall and wonder if it's one of Dr. Yang's patients. The waiting room is filled with one shaggy dog, two cottontail rabbits, a guinea pig, a fat hamster, and a black mouse climbing up the arm of his owner.

I peek into the turtle carrier that Dad and I made this morning before school. Mom doesn't know it yet, but she donated a plastic container and a blue towel. Dad cut holes in the top, and we misted Bert with water before we left. Then I added a worm and some leftover squash.

"You okay?" I say.

Bert pokes his neck out when he hears my voice. Then quickly tucks it back in when the shaggy dog starts barking.

The door opens, and a mom and her son come in. "My gerbil just had babies. Lots and lots of babies," the boy says proudly as he shows the inside of his shoebox to a woman with a bun who's behind a counter. As I'm watching the little boy, who reminds me of Charlie, I feel something tug at my right sneaker. When I look down, there's a very large turtle nibbling on my bright-green shoelace.

I hear a man laugh. "Oh, that's Pepper, the office's sulcata tortoise. He loves colored shoelaces." The man reroutes the tortoise and shows us into room 1.

Dr. Yang is waiting in there with her spearmint breath and parrot charm necklace. "So, Maggie, who do we have here?"

"This is Bert," I say. "An eastern painted turtle. I found him over by the pond near the trap field."

"May I?" She holds out her hand, and I put my new friend in her palm.

"He's beautiful. I love his orange belly and his distinctive marking." She points to the heart-shaped spot on his shell.

"Me too. What do you think the marking is from?"

She runs her hand over his shell. "Most likely he got into it with a coyote."

"Is he okay?" I ask.

She nods. "He's tough. And his shell is strong."

I look over at Dad, who's smiling. I know he wants me to be able to keep Bert, too.

"Some things you need to know about this little guy," Dr. Yang says. "He's surprisingly fast and well camouflaged." She points to his brown shell. "If you bring him out of his habitat, don't take your eyes off him. He can move between twenty and thirty feet in only thirty seconds."

"Wow! I knew he was speedy, but that's super-speedy! Anything else?" I ask.

"Wash your hands after you hold Bert, clean his home regularly, don't put him in a sink or bathtub, and steer him away from the kitchen. Also, when your dad called to make this appointment, he mentioned there's a new baby in the house. Keep him out of the baby's room and off her things."

"Got it." I give her and Dad a thumbs-up.

"We used to feed my turtle cooked hamburger and greens," my dad says. "Is that something this guy would like?"

"Sure. Mix in some flowers and lettuce, and it'll be a feast."

We all laugh.

She puts Bert back into his carrier. "Take good care of him, love him a lot, and he'll be around for a long time. These guys can live up to fifty years."

My whole body springs into happy mode.

11

Mr. Spud

When we get home from the vet, I tell my little brother that Bert is officially a forever member of the Hunt family. "Yay!" he says, jumping up and down. "Did you know that Principal James has a turtle in his office and his name is Mr. Spud? Maybe they can be friends."

"Maybe," I say.

"Did you know that rats can't throw up?"

I shake my head no.

Charlie blows Bert a kiss, and I return my turtle to a rock in his tub. I tell Charlie to go wash his hands. When he scampers back in, he has a tennis ball. It's Break the Record Week at school, and he's trying to beat the class best for the number of times in a row a student can bounce a tennis ball without dropping it. He told me the current record is fifty-two. He's at twenty-three bounces when his ball rolls under my bed.

My whole body freezes.

He reaches for my blanket.

"Don't!" I yell.

Charlie's big brown eyes open wide.

"Drop the blanket and leave my room!"

He doesn't move.

"Now!" I scream.

His eyes leak. "But my ball is under your bed. Let me just get it, and then—"

"Get out!" I feel the heat spread across my face.

He darts out of my room. I close my door and exhale the angry knot twisted inside of me. I look under my bed and see the ball next to my boxes. I snatch it, open my door, and toss it in the hall.

Sorry, Bear.

The words echo in my head, but I don't say them.

I grab my boxes and tuck into the corner of my

room. Surrounded by cardboard. And memories. I add small threads from Izzie's baby blanket.

A keepsake.

To have.

Forever.

There's a knock on the door.

I quickly slide my boxes back under my bed and pull the comforter down low.

Mom walks in with a pile of clean clothes in her arms. She puts them on my desk next to my geometry homework, my trap vest, and the last pile of clean clothes she brought in. "I heard you yelling. You need to apologize to your brother and clean up this place."

Can't everyone just leave my stuff alone?

"I'll say I'm sorry to Charlie." I look around my bedroom. "But I like my room this way. It's cozy. Lived-in."

"It's a mess."

I shake my head. "It's not a mess. I just have a different way of organizing than you do."

"This is not organized," she says. "Either you clean it, I clean it, or we clean it together. Up to you."

None of the options really work for me, especially the last two. "I'll apologize now and clean after I walk Batman. I told Ava I'd stop by, and Sam is meeting us there."

Ava lives around the block in the brick ranch house on the corner. Mom agrees to the plan, but makes me promise to text her when I get to Ava's.

I pop into Charlie's room. He's lining up his plastic toy animals in a parade across his floor.

I sit next to him.

"Did you know your face gets red like Gramps's tomatoes when you're mad?" he says.

I shake my head.

He puts his hands on his hips. "I don't like when you yell at me with your red face."

"I'm really sorry." *My mad flipped on when you moved toward my boxes under my bed*, I want to say. *And I couldn't stuff it back in until you were far away from my things.* But I can't tell him that, because *I* don't even understand it.

In a small voice he says, "I forgive you. But I'm still a little sad about it."

"That's fair." Then I hold out my arms. "Love you huge, Bear."

He moves closer, snuggles in, and hugs my neck.

I leave him and his parade, and head with Batman to Ava's house. On the way, I give some love to Clover, the Altmans' floppy sheepdog, before turning down Willow Lane and ringing Ava's very loud doorbell. When I get to her room, I text Mom. Promise kept.

Ava's working on a project for the school coding club, called Find Me—think dog sweater with a tracking device that links to an app on a phone to locate a lost pet. Apparently, they started it after Bruno, the club president's hairless Chinese crested dog, went missing.

"How's it going?" I say.

She gives me a thumbs-up, but her eyes stay locked on the computer screen. She told me when we met in second grade that she wants to be a coder, like her mom. She's been saving her money for college since she started Walk with Me, her neighborhood dog-walking business. Sometimes, Batman and

I join her on her walks with Max, Brady, and Maple, the beagle, golden retriever, and bichon that live on her block.

I think someone should make an app like this for people you love who can't remember where they live. Like Nana that time she got lost. Really lost. It wasn't long after Forgot-Me Day. Mom and Dad had to call Officer Daniel Scott to help. Eventually they found her at the G & J Gas Station, eating a cherry slush. I never even knew she liked slushes.

I peek over Ava's shoulder. I don't know how to code. To me, it looks like a bunch of random words and letters mixed with a lot of math stuff. Batman yawns and lies down. On top of Mr. Koala.

"Hey, watch out," Ava says to Batman, sliding Mr. Koala out from under him.

"You should really take better care of him. I mean, his ears are shredded, and he has three holes in his belly."

"That's called love," Ava says, laughing.

I plunk down on Ava's bed.

"Where's Sam?" I ask her. "I thought she was coming."

"She was. But her parents said she had to go to this award thing for her sister."

"Again?"

Ava nods.

"Hey, Maggie!" one of Ava's brothers shouts as another one chases him down the hall. I wave, and they disappear, arguing about who's stronger. Faster. Taller.

Ava shuts her door.

I inch closer to my best friend. "I need to tell you something. But you have to promise not to think I'm a horrible person. Okay?"

"I promise." We clap our hands three times, knock our fists twice, and lock pinkies. We've been doing that since Ava told me in second grade that she sleeps with the lights on because she's scared of the dark.

The air around me is ready to collect my words, but they're not coming out.

"Well, are you going to tell me?" Ava asks.

Maybe I shouldn't.

I look down at Snoring Batman and then back to Ava.

"Spit it out," she says.

With one big gulp I say, "I kind of hope Izzie doesn't get adopted." Then I hold my breath and wait for my best friend not to think I'm the worst person ever.

"Isn't that the whole point?" Ava asks, scratching behind Batman's ears.

"I guess. Sort of," I say.

"I mean, I thought your family was just taking care of her *until* she gets adopted."

"But think about it. If she doesn't get adopted, then maybe we can keep her. You know, forever."

"Did your parents say that?"

"Not exactly." Then the truth slips out. "No."

"Honestly, I don't get what you think is so great about having a family loaded with siblings," Ava says as her brothers throw a ball against their shared wall. "Plus, I don't want you to get your hopes up. Remember what that lady said: Izzie isn't yours."

"But that's just it. I want her to be mine. For always."

Ava hugs me tight. "Look, you're not a horrible person. Your heart's just too big. Remember when you begged your mom to adopt that smelly stray dog that followed us to school? And last summer, you wanted to go to that place where they had the tornado, so you could help find all the lost pets."

I wasn't allowed to adopt Cocoa the stray dog, but we did give him a bath, and bones that tasted like chicken, and then drove him to the animal shelter. And while Mom had said it wasn't safe enough yet to travel where the tornado had hit, Dad and I made a podcast for his show that had tips for finding lost pets after a natural disaster. Lots of people sent emails thanking us and some even sent photos with their found dogs and cats, and a rabbit named Oreo.

"And you just brought home a turtle," Ava says.

I texted Ava a picture of Bert swimming in the plastic tub last night with the message:

Meet the newest member of the family.

On the walk home, I wonder about too-big hearts and apps that can find lost nanas.

12

Hot Dogs, Mustard, and Diapers

The next day, Gramps and Charlie pick me up from school. Gramps's car smells like the hike up Ridge Mountain. I think it's the green cardboard tree dangling from his rearview mirror, which he got to hide the stink from the cigars he's not supposed to be smoking. I move the bakery box filled with chocolate doughnuts that's on my seat and hand it to my grandfather.

He and Nana always ate one doughnut a day for breakfast. Every week, Nana would walk into The Baking Room and without saying one word, Ida, the owner, would hand her fourteen chocolate doughnuts, in a box tied with string. Now, Gramps buys his own doughnuts.

He gives us each some chocolatey goodness and winks.

"Thanks for the nun fart," Charlie says, cracking up.

Gramps nods and laughs. "I'm not sure how Charlie found this out," Gramps says, "but in France, doughnuts are called '*pets de nonne*,' which translates to 'nun farts.'"

The laughter bounces off the walls of my grandfather's tan Chevy.

We're on a run to the store for more diapers. Dad was going to come with us, but he had to interview a guy named Tyrone Jefferson for his podcast. Jefferson's some big-deal scientist who's researching a genetically engineered crop that he says could end world hunger. Sadly, I don't think Gramps's chocolate doughnuts are part of Jefferson's master farming plan.

When we get to Box Mart, we head to aisle four and find diapers for the tiniest ones. After that,

I'm ready to leave, but Charlie spies the aisle with trucks, and Gramps wants to check out what's on sale.

We stroll all over the store with our diapers and our cart and a yellow truck that Charlie somehow got Gramps to agree to buy for him. Gramps pokes in the sale bins, humming to the Marvin Gaye hits playing over the loudspeakers. He finds black and gray and blue argyle socks at 50 percent off, towels at 10 percent off, and large tubs of mayonnaise—buy one, get one free. I successfully convince him that he doesn't eat enough tuna salad to get through even one tub before it expires, but can't convince him that he doesn't need the socks or the towels.

Gramps turns to me as we pass aisle seven—pet supplies. "Does Bert need anything? There's lots of pet stuff on sale."

"Actually, some turtle food would be great. I think Mom and Dad might start noticing that I've been stealing the romaine lettuce and squash. And even some of the leftover hamburger."

We stock up on all things turtle, pay, and head over to the hot-dog counter. This is the best part of

Box Mart. They sell giant hot dogs in big doughy buns. I load mine with relish and onions, and Charlie fills his with yellow mustard and bacon bits. Then we all slide into the plastic chairs at one of the sticky red tables.

After one giant bite, Charlie has mustard dripping down his chin. I hand him a napkin. "I think Mom and Dad should keep Izzie," I say.

"Hmm," Gramps says.

"Did you know astronauts ate bacon on the moon?" Charlie says.

My grandfather gives him a thumbs-up.

I look at my brother and then at Gramps. "I think *you* should tell our parents that we should keep her. I mean, they'll listen to you."

He laughs. "What makes you believe that I think you should keep Izzie?"

"I heard you singing Nana's favorite song to her the night we brought her home," I say, finishing the last bite of my hot dog and tucking my napkin into my pocket.

When we get back home, Gramps and Charlie unpack the stuff, and Mom's waiting for me in the family room. Something feels off. And it's not just the ugly painting she bought and hung because it matched the honey-colored wallpaper.

"I got a call from Rita," Mom says. "The birth parents have selected an adoptive couple, and I need to bring Isabelle back to Rita's office so she can give her to her forever family."

"When?"

"Saturday."

So now I know.

Forever ends tomorrow.

13

Love You, Little Bean

The panic rises from the place that holds my forever good-byes.

To Nana.

And now, Izzie.

I hug this little human who smells like powder, and a tear slips out. I don't want to let her go. Don't want to be forgotten. I want to teach her how to ride a two-wheeler, hold her hand when she crosses the street, and be annoyed when she borrows my favorite sunflower T-shirt. I want to be her sister for keeps.

"I want her to stay."

"She can't, Maggie," Mom says. Then she tells

me about the adoptive couple, Asher and Maya. They're from Louisiana. They have happy smiles and big hearts and want a family. More than anything.

Mom reminds me what an important thing we're doing.

But it's not working.

I don't want to be reminded.

I want Izzie.

"We should keep her," I say. "I'll babysit. And change diapers."

Mom takes my hands and, in a voice wrapped in love, says, "First, we're not approved for adoption. Only foster care. Second, even if we got approval, Dad and I can't work and care for a newborn, along with Charlie, Dillon, and you."

"Yes, you can. I'll help," I say.

"It's not possible. And it's not our job. Our job as a short-term foster family has always only been to love and care for these babies who need us. And then to give them to their forever families. Remember?"

I do, but I don't care. Another tear sneaks out, and Mom tucks me in her arms.

I take my baby sister to her room. Door open. A Rita Rule. I look into Izzie's ocean-blue eyes. We sit in the wooden rocker, and I read *I Love You More*. Then I read it again so she can remember my voice. Maybe when I'm twenty and she's eight and hears me ordering a chocolate doughnut at The Baking Room, she'll recognize the beat and sound of my voice. And then, just maybe, she'll remember me.

I pull her close. I feel her breath on my cheek. I hum and look out the window. The moon is bright and round and low in the dark sky. If I stretch out my arm, it looks like I can touch it. "This is our moon," I tell Izzie. "Ours to share. If we see the same moon night after night in the sky, then we can stay connected. Be connected." I kiss her sweet head. "Love you, Little Bean."

Then I stuff the binkie with the green frog into my pocket.

For keeps.

14

Blue Glitter and the Moon

I put Izzie in the bassinet and head to my room. I open one of the cardboard boxes from under my bed and survey my stuff. The gecko necklace from Nana. The Bert rock. Some baby-blanket threads. The tassel from Nana's favorite pomegranate scarf. Sticks from a hike up Ridge Mountain, a walk with Charlie, and Wade's Pond. Gum wrappers. Three bendy straws. One yellow sock. And photos of Izzie. (Dad let me print them on his special color printer, and I made two copies of each. One for Izzie's Life Book and one for me.)

I drop in my sister's frog binkie. It lies on top like a cherry on a sundae. I wonder what I'll do when I run out of space in this box. Don't think any more boxes can fit under my bed *or* in my closet. The last things I stuffed in the closet boxes were the green bath mat, my favorite hairbrush with the missing bristles that Mom said was garbage, an empty cardboard box with the string from The Bakery Room, and a bottle of Nana's perfume.

After Nana died, we sat shiva. It's a thing Jewish people do after someone passes away. Dad says it's so the family feels the love all around them. I'm not totally convinced. During Nana's shiva, lots of people came to our house with cookies and casseroles, and told me they loved Nana huge, but then hugged me too tight and said confusing things like, "It's for the best," and "She's better off."

While I was trying to understand what they meant I snuck into Gramps and Nana's room and slipped a bottle of her perfume into my pocket. That night I put it in the box. It was a little piece of her. When I close my eyes and hold the bottle, I can still smell her.

Roses. With a hint of cherry.

I grab my Idea Book. Dad gave one to each of us—me, Charlie, and Dillon. It's black with yellow stripes, and on the cover it says GO ON, CHANGE THE WORLD! He got the notebooks to promote his new podcast. Dad says we can all make the world brighter. One little thing at a time. Mom says brightness comes from a light bulb. And a business plan. I'm not sure, but either way, I love my notebook. It reminds me of a bumblebee. Minus the stinger and the buzz. I grab my favorite purple pen, the one I got at the arcade with my Skee-Ball tickets, and start writing.

Today's Ideas to Change the World

1. Convince Mom and Dad to keep Izzie.
2. Give Bert lots of lettuce and worms.
3. Eat chocolate.
4. Keep everyone out of my stuff.

Under my list, I draw a picture of Izzie. After a while, I spy Charlie standing in my doorway, watching me sketch.

"What are you doing?" he asks.

"Nothing," I say.

Then he points to my notebook.

"Oh, drawing a picture of Izzie in that book Dad gave me."

Charlie darts down the hall. When he comes back, he hands me his notebook. Most pages have a misspelled word and a picture.

Knd.
Brocli
Lov
Baf
Smle
Bike

"These are great, Bear."

"Dad says I should use my book to think of ways to make the world happier," Charlie says.

I look through his pages and stop at the picture he drew of himself in the tub surrounded by all his dinosaurs. "How does taking a bath make the world better?"

"If you don't smell stinky, that's good. Right?" he asks, smelling his armpits.

I nod and hug my clean little brother.

Then he hands me a card.

"Is this part of your change-the-world plan?" I ask.

He shakes his head. "No, this is for Izzie."

The card's shaped like a moon and covered in a thick coat of blue sparkles.

My heart squeezes tight as I take his hand and walk him into Izzie's room to give our baby sister her card.

That night, I tell Charlie the story of the moon. How it connects us all.

He draws a moon on one of the pages in his book and tells me the moon isn't round, it's shaped like an egg. Then he tells me that he thinks there are certain times of year when the moon's covered in blue glitter.

That's when I realize that no matter how many random facts my little brother knows, he's still just six.

15

Good-Bye Day

It's been almost twenty-four hours since Mom shared the news.

Twenty-four hours since I learned how long forever is.

Today is Good-Bye Day.

I hand Mom all the photos I've taken for the Life Book. And she hands me Izzie. Eight days of being Little Bean's big sister and now it's over. Just like that, the smell of love that's flooded every cell in my body will disappear like a mountain in the fog. I hold her close and sing "Lullaby Blue." I soak in every detail. I want to remember her tuft of acorn-brown hair, her soft skin, and her big blue eyes. I want to remember what love this big feels like.

"It's time, Maggie," Dad says from the doorway. We need to leave for trap.

I hand my baby sister to my mom.

I hate forever good-byes.

Last night before bed, I campaigned again to keep Izzie. "It's not fair," I said. "Charlie wants to be a big brother. I want a little sister." My hands flew all over the place. "Look, even Dillon likes her! When he thinks no one's around, he talks to her. I heard him."

The room went silent. My parents exchanged a look. Not the good kind.

But I wasn't giving up. "You said our job was to love her, and we did. And we do. How can we just give her back? Like none of this happened. Like she's not my baby sister."

"Maggie, our job was always *only* short-term foster care. We were never going to be Izzie's forever family," Dad said.

"But I don't love in tiny doses," I said, my cheeks wet.

The mist settles on the treetops. I don't want to get out of the truck. I hate today.

Izzie is leaving, and so is one of the Original Five.

I see Mason standing by the red building. Ava, Sam, and Gracie are huddled together nearby. Sam's got her hair wrapped around her finger, and I over-hear Ava say that Max the beagle tried to chase two squirrels up a tree on their walk this morning.

Dad calls us together and officially welcomes Mason to our squad. Everyone knows him. Before today, he was part of Eagle Eyes but shooting with the intermediate squad. Apparently, he's been prac-ticing. Because now he's an intermediate advanced, and the fifth member of our almost-all-girl squad.

"Will Belle be able to rejoin our squad?" Gracie asks.

Belle texted all of us last night. She's now shooting with Mason's old squad. I miss her already. Especially since we don't go to the same school anymore. In fifth grade, she transferred to an all-girls school. Trap was our time. Together.

"The only thing we're focusing on are the five members of the squad who are here today. And making *everyone* feel welcome," Dad says.

It doesn't work. The air's still thick and filled with uncomfortable things not said. I rub my arms to erase the goose bumps that have cropped up. Then Dad reminds us of the three safety rules before we get into position: Action open. Finger off the trigger. Gun pointed in a safe direction.

As squad leader, I head to position one. Followed by Mason, Ava, Sam, and Gracie. I see Gracie's purple socks peeking out from under her pants.

I think about Izzie, and a sinking feeling of sadness burrows in.

I shout the last safety rule, "Eyes and ears!" and look around to be sure everyone's got their safety goggles on and ear protection in. Ava's earplugs match her green socks. Mine don't match anything.

They were a gift from Dad, a special moldable yellow-and-green pair.

I raise my shotgun, shoulder it, and press my cheek hard against the wood stock, then yell, "Pull!"

The neon-orange disc hurls by, but my mind is stuck on good-byes. Silence fills the space around me as the disc floats in the air and then hits the ground, untouched.

Next round, I miss again. And again. The sadness tugs at me.

After five missed shots, I move to the second position and wait for the nod from Ava in position one to be sure everyone is ready.

"Pull!" Miss. Can't concentrate. The clay neon disc sails away from me untouched. Again.

I end up with a 10/25. One of my worst scores. Ever.

No one does well, and Dad calls us in for a pep talk. But everyone still looks miserable. That's the thing about those talks. They don't really work.

When Dad and I get to his truck, I hear a gruff rumble of a voice. It's coming from a linebacker-size man with a bushy beard, wearing a Bruins cap.

"My son's not going to be a part of some mediocre girls' squad."

The words swallow the breeze blowing across the parking lot.

"Ray, this is the best group of shooters we have at Fish, Fur, and Fly," Dad says.

"Didn't look like the best group of anything," Mason's father says, moving next to his son.

My head drops.

"Look, your son was invited to join this squad," Dad says, "and head with us to the state tournament at the end of the season."

Mason's dad steps closer, finger pointing in my dad's face. "There's no way—"

"Dad, stop!" Mason says. Then he opens the door to the gray truck parked next to us, sits in the front passenger seat, and crosses his arms.

Welcome to the almost-all-girl trapshooting squad.

16

Ruby Red

On the drive home, I don't want to talk about how poorly I shot, Mason's dad, or our no-longer-all-girl squad. My insides are filled with a missing that can't be fixed with words. When I walk through the bright-blue door, our house is Izzie-empty.

I kick off my muddy shoes and throw my trap vest over the chair, and my Eagle Eyes cap on my bed. Dad got caps for the whole *new* squad. Pine-green. Yellow writing. Then I follow him to the gun safe to store my shotgun. Batman runs over and licks my face. I hand him a peanut-butter-flavored bone and nestle into his fur, hoping his dog love will swallow my sadness.

I leave Dad and head upstairs. I open my playlist and scroll until I find the song I need. The words of Grace Potter's "Timekeeper" fill my room as I sink onto the floor next to my newest box. It's growing. I drop in a button from Bud the Bear. I rub the threads I kept from Izzie's white blanket between my fingers. They smell like powder. I hurt. All the way through.

I think of Izzie's deep-blue eyes and tiny nose. I think about her birth parents. I wonder if they miss Izzie in that place where grown-up explanations and talk can't fix. I wipe my cheeks and close my box.

I do my push-ups, then my pull-ups on the chin-up bar Dad hung on my doorframe and wait for the exercise to make me feel better. It doesn't. I look around and realize I don't want to be here anymore. I tell Dad I'm heading to Gramps's house and grab my bike. His house is only two blocks away.

The door's open. It's always open. Through the window, I see my grandfather in the backyard. He's wearing the plaid flannel shirt we gave him for his seventieth birthday last year. I walk down the hall, through the kitchen, and past the symphonic *tick-tock* of his clock collection. The bright-orange mixing-bowl clock is my favorite. Gramps spies me and waves me outside.

He stands tall and wipes the sweat with his gardening gloves. I go in for the giant moose hug.

"I miss her already," I say.

"I know," he says. "Me too." Then he points toward the tomato plants. "Want to help?"

I nod.

"Remember, twist and pull," he says. "Gently," he adds, as if I haven't been helping with this garden since I could walk. Although I'm not sure *helping* has always been the right word for it. Sometimes it was just eating—ripe tomatoes, basil, cucumbers, and really everything. My favorite are the little yellow tomatoes. I love the way their sweetness bursts in my mouth.

"Got it." I twirl the bright-red Big Girl tomatoes and wonder who gets to name these. Big Girl. Big Boy. Green Zebra. Enchantment. Big Beef. Big Mama. "If you could name a tomato, what would you call it?"

Gramps stands straight, his crystal-blue eyes gazing up toward the sun and then right at me. "Hmm. I think I'd name it Ruby Red." He smiles.

"After Nana?" This was her garden. Ever since I was little, this has been my happy place. Nana said it was magical. Today, I hope she's right. My heart could use some special magic.

Gramps nods. Nana's real name was Ruth. She hated that name but loved her fire-engine-red hair, so everyone called her Ruby. Gramps says I look just like her.

Every April in their kitchen with the yellow-and-green-striped wallpaper, Nana would start the seeds. I'd fill a Dixie cup with dirt, she'd hand me a seed, I'd poke a hole in the dirt, slide the seed down, cover it up, give it a drink of water, and she'd write the name of the plant on the outside. Then we'd watch and wait. That was always the hardest part. I'm a terrible waiter. I'd stop by every day to see my plants. Frustration would fill me until I'd see a sprig of green. Then pure happiness.

I think this garden is like my boxes. A place

where memories last and specks of happiness live forever.

"Ruby Red sounds like a good one," I say. "I'd name those little sweet ones Izzies," I add, a slip of sadness seeping out.

Gramps sits on the wooden box that holds Nana's gardening tools. I plop down on the ground next to him. "You never even liked tomatoes or gardening," I say.

"I know. Gardening was your grandmother's thing." He pauses to take a drink from his water bottle that says BEST GRANDPA EVER. "Then Doughnut Day happened, and I found myself wanting to be out here."

I look at his sun-kissed, wrinkled face. He has three long lines etched across his forehead. Doughnut Day was a Sunday, not long after Forgot-Me Day. Mom and I brought the usual order of chocolate doughnuts to Gramps, since Nana couldn't get to The Baking Room anymore and Gramps wouldn't leave her alone in the house. Gramps showed her the doughnuts. His smile was bright, like we'd brought the one thing that could fix her, the one thing that could bring her back to all of us. But instead of biting into her favorite dessert, she said, "I don't like doughnuts." Gramps tried to do what he always did. Talk to her. Remind her. But she started saying things that didn't make sense. She called him by her brother's name. Nana's brother had died two years earlier. Then a giant sadness draped over all the uneaten doughnuts.

"I feel close to her out here," Gramps said.

I get that. I lay my head on my grandfather's knee, thinking about Izzie and Nana. And the giant missing.

17

Dance Party

When Gramps leaves for his weekly game of bridge, I text Dad to let him know I'm stopping at Belle's. I'm not ready to go back to a house without a sister.

I lean my bike against Belle's garage. Before I go in, I take out my phone and find my favorite photo of Izzie. The one that Dad took when I was holding her that first night. Her tiny body fit so perfectly in my arms. I wonder how it's possible to love someone so completely in just eight days.

I inhale big, put my phone away, and ring the doorbell. Belle's mom opens the door with a gigantic hug and a very enthusiastic hello.

"I'm sorry my dad moved Belle from our squad," I say.

"Oh, dear. Don't you worry about that. Belle may have switched squads, but so long as she's still shooting trap for Fish, Fur, and Fly, she's just fine. Honest. And if she's good, I'm good," she says, followed by a smile filled with lots of superwhite teeth.

I wonder if Belle really is fine. Then I hear music blaring from her room, and when I open the door, she's dancing on top of her bed, holding her hamster, Linus.

"Dance party," she says, motioning for me to join her.

But I don't want to. Not now. "I wish you were still on our squad. It's not the same without you."

She pops Linus in his plastic exercise ball, turns up the music, and continues dancing.

"How's the new squad?"

"Good," she says. "Coach Aiden is helping me with my shot."

"You okay?" I ask, sitting on the floor with Linus.

She nods to the beat.

"I promise to keep asking my dad if you can come back. I mean, that's how it should be. All of us together."

Belle turns the music down and hops off her once dance floor, now messy bed. "Don't keep asking him." She walks over to me. "I like where I am. There's less pressure. And I'm still part of Eagle Eyes, just a different squad. I'm good. I promise."

She pushes her bedroom door closed so Linus doesn't roll down the hallway. "What about you? Are you all right? You look really sad."

I tell her that Izzie is gone. She slides next to me on the floor and takes my hands. I wonder if she can feel my sadness through my fingers. We watch Linus rolling in circles and listen to music until I need to leave.

On my ride home, I think about Nana and Izzie and Belle.

And wonder if there will ever be a time when good-byes don't leave a gaping hole in my heart.

18

Change of Plans

Charlie's in my room with Bert and Batman when I get home from Belle's. I rub behind my dog's ears while Bert nibbles a worm Charlie found for him outside.

"Did you know starfish can turn their stomachs inside out?" Charlie asks.

Sometimes random facts help me forget the missing.

But then I hear the front door creak open, and I remember.

I dart downstairs. Two steps at a time. I want to know everything about Izzie's forever family. Are they kind and loving? And happy? Do they know Izzie likes to be held high on the shoulder and rocked when she's crying? Did they like the photos I took for her Life Book?

When I get to the bottom of the stairs, Mom's standing in the hallway on the plum-colored carpet.

Holding Izzie.

I stop.

Run over and hug my mom and baby sister.

"I thought I'd never see her again," I say.

"There's been a change of plans."

"Why didn't you call Dad or me?"

"Couldn't reach you guys at trap. There's no reception there. Then my phone died." She holds up her silver case to show the black screen. "I thought I'd just finish my errands and come tell you in person."

"Tell me what?"

"Izzie needs to stay with us a little longer."

Happiness wraps around me like Nana's afghan.

I hold our tiny human in my arms and kiss her soft head. "Wait. Why?"

"There was a hurricane in Louisiana where the adoptive couple is from. The airports are closed, and the roads are flooded. They can't get out."

My breath catches in the back of my throat.

Did I put this in the universe when I wished for her to stay? Did I do this?

Guilt crashes down on me.

19

Just In Case

I try to reach Ava, but I remember she's with her mom at some coding camp for the rest of the weekend. I need to talk to her. I need to know I didn't cause the storm with all my wishing and hoping and universe sharing. *Is this my fault?*

I spend all of the next day at home. Charlie and I build an animal parade that stretches across two rooms and read four books together. Over and over again. The house is quiet. Dad's with Dillon at his travel basketball tournament, and Mom's working with a student who's applying early to college.

After takeout fried chicken, I finish my geometry homework and move into Izzie's room. She falls asleep with Bud the Bear watching over her. I listen to her breathing and snuggle under the afghan, hoping it'll make me feel less responsible for the bad thing. I close my eyes and drift to sleep. In my dreams, I'm lost. Can't find my way home to the bright-blue door no matter how many times I start over.

When I wake, it's still nighttime. I head to my room and my newest box. I use my flashlight to peek inside. Everything's there. My body relaxes, and I fall back to sleep.

Batman licks my face to wake me for school the next morning. I get dressed and, on my way downstairs, stop in to visit Izzie. But she's not in her bassinet.

When I get to the kitchen, Mom's yawning, with a very large mug of coffee in her hand. "This little one has been awake for hours." Mom's eyes are puffy and red. I give her and Izzie a kiss goodbye, grab a package of peanut-butter crackers, and text Ava to meet me by the weeping willow tree in the front of the school.

I'm halfway there when I realize I left my

geometry homework on my bed. I text Ava that I'll be late, sprint back to the house, and race up to my room.

I'm panting when I open my bedroom door.

To my mom.

Cleaning my room.

"What are you doing?" I ask, my words colored with anger.

"Putting the stuff away that you said you'd clean up and didn't." Her pajamas have spit-up on the left shoulder.

"Well, stop! This isn't your room! It's mine!" I feel the heat rise from the soles of my feet.

"You need to settle down. We have rules in this house, Maggie. Respect is one of them. The other is keeping your room clean."

My anger twists and tightens.

"It is. Mostly. Clean." I'd put a bunch of my stuff away. The other day. Just like I promised. The truth is, I don't get why a clean room is such a big deal. But I need this conversation to end. I swallow the voice that wants to scream, and instead say, "Fine, I'll put *all* my things away, if you agree to leave them alone." I grab my homework and shove it in my bag. "But right now, I need to go back to school so I'm not late," I say, hoping tardiness outweighs cleanliness in order of importance to my mom.

"I want this room cleaned when you get back from school. Today." She stares at me.

I nod. I'll agree to almost anything to get her out of my bedroom. Away from my stuff.

I run to school, the angry burning in my chest. I text Ava that I'm on the way, and when I get there, she's waiting for me at our tree. I look at my watch. We still have time before the first bell. I slip next to her, and she hands me a bag of barbecue potato chips.

"Breakfast of champions," I say.

She smiles. "It was this or the oatmeal stuck to the bottom of the pot."

I give her half of my peanut-butter crackers.

"What's going on?" she asks.

I don't want to talk about the weird mad that took over my brain when I saw my mom cleaning my room. Instead, I focus on the reason I was up in the middle of the night. "Do you think wishing for one thing to happen can make something else happen? Something bad?"

"Um, what are you talking about?" She nods toward my water, and I hand her the bottle.

"Izzie."

"What about her?"

"She's still here." Kids and teachers start to fill in around us. I spy Ms. López, my English teacher, wheeling her ginormous flowered bag. It's like a traveling bookstore.

"Congrats! That's what you wanted," Ava says. "So why do you look so freaked-out? You're doing that weird thing with your lip."

In a small voice I say, "The reason Izzie is still with my family is because there was a big hurricane in Louisiana."

"I saw that on the news," Ava says. "People were using canoes to get around the streets. You should tell your dad to run that story again about finding lost pets on his podcast. I bet there are lots of dogs and cats that can't find their owners."

"I'm worried it was my fault."

My best friend stares at me. "The hurricane is

obviously a really bad thing, but I'm not getting how it could be your fault. You don't even live in Louisiana."

"Remember when I told you that I didn't want Izzie to get adopted because I wanted her to stay with me?"

"Yeah."

"Well, I put that wish into the universe, and now I'm worried that I made this terrible thing happen."

"Are you serious?" Ava takes the last bite of her peanut-butter cracker and a big gulp of my water.

I don't answer, because my words weave with blame and a heavy dose of I'm-a-terrible-person.

"Unless you're from another planet where you can harness the magic of the sun or stars or unicorns, you don't have the power to make stuff happen. Or not happen." She laughs.

"What about putting things out there in the universe? I mean, I did that. I asked the universe for her to stay."

"I don't believe in that stuff. You can't just wish for something to happen, and then it magically does. I mean, if that were true, why isn't there world peace?"

"I never thought of it that way."

The bell rings.

On the walk into the middle school, there's a part of me that still believes in wishing. And the universe. So I squeeze my eyes shut and silently hope for everyone in Louisiana to be okay. I might not have any real power, but just in case.

20

Frog or Lizard

Ava and I follow the trail of kids into school. She heads down the hall to her locker, and I go to mine. I grab my English notebook from my backpack, then look around to make sure no one's paying attention. I quickly open my locker, slide in my bag, and slam the door closed. But it snags on something and springs open.

"What do you have in there?" It's Sam, who's now standing next to me. "It's totally overflowing," she says.

I close my locker before she can see any more. "Oh, that stuff is for an assignment in art class."

Ava comes over. "What smells?"

I shrug and head to English.

Ms. López is standing by her messy Mom-wouldn't-approve desk in room 404. Just above her chair hangs a sign that says SO MANY THINGS ARE POSSIBLE JUST AS LONG AS YOU DON'T KNOW THEY'RE IMPOSSIBLE.—*THE PHANTOM TOLLBOOTH* BY NORTON JUSTER

Ms. López is a big believer in the power of positive thinking. That's what she told us on the first day of seventh grade. Some days, I believe her. Today I'm not sure.

She moves to the front of the class, two fingers in the air. We're supposed to stop talking. It almost works, except for Lysander, who's bragging about the goals he scored during yesterday's soccer game against the Falcons.

Ms. López waits until he stops talking long enough for her to assign partners for our poetry-unit project. Mason is mine. When I look over, he nods, his dark hair hanging in front of his eyes. Then Ms. López writes the assignment on the board: *Beyond Poetry: How and why people use poetic language in the world.*

Keisha's hand shoots in the air. "What's 'poetic language'?"

Ms. López moves to the front of the class. "Good question. Similes, metaphors, hyperboles, alliterations, puns, and personifications are all part of the poetic language. I want you and your partner to search songs, ads, newspapers, menus, the internet—anywhere in your regular life—to find examples."

She fills the big table at the front of our classroom with all sorts of that stuff, then gives us the next twenty minutes to begin looking. "This is just the start. The project will continue for the next few weeks."

"What do you want to look through first?" I ask Mason.

He shrugs and stuffs his hands in his pockets. He's wearing a Patriots championship T-shirt. I have the same one at home.

"Let's check out the newspaper," I say.

Mason grabs a copy of the *Boston Globe* from the table. When he opens it up, I see an ad for Becker's All-Natural Baby Formula, and my mind shifts to Izzie and my box. My stomach swirls, hoping Mom has kept her promise. That she hasn't found my stuff. Touched my stuff. Cleaned my stuff. My breath tightens.

Then I hear Mason's voice. "Oh, here's a pun in an ad for Freddie's Car Repair. It says, 'We will shock and exhaust you.'"

"Good one," I say, squeezing a smile out while Mason writes our pun on the sheet Ms. López gave us.

I scour the rest of the paper, hoping to squash my worry with poetic language. Then I turn to Mason. "Hey, sorry about Saturday."

"It's okay. One time, I shot a 5/25. An hour later, I was at the hospital having an appendicitis."

"Actually, I wasn't talking about my score. Although I did have one of my worst days ever. I was talking about your dad."

"Oh, that," he says, flipping to the sports section.

"Maybe if I don't stink next practice, your dad will be happier. You know, he'll see that we're a really strong team."

"Doubt it."

"Why?" I dig in my pocket and hand Mason one

of the two mints I grabbed when we left Sam's Seafood Alley the last time I went there. It was just after Charlie announced that a cockroach can live for nine days without its head. "Don't you think your dad will feel better about the new squad if he sees we're good?"

"Not likely. He hates everything about trap. And being on an all-girl squad makes it worse."

"Obviously, we're not an all-girl anything anymore. Belle was cut to make room for you. Remember?" I unwrap the other green-and-white-striped candy and pop it into my mouth.

"Whatever."

"It's not a whatever thing. It's a huge thing."

He doesn't say anything.

"What does your mom think?" I ask, flipping the mint in circles with my tongue.

He looks at me. Unease wedges between us. "Just don't tell your friends what happened the other day in the parking lot with my dad."

I'm quiet.

"Okay?" he asks.

I nod. Then I catch a glimpse of a sketch pad

sticking out of his backpack. The cover's ripped off, and the page is filled with amazing cartoonlike drawings.

"Those are really cool." I point to his bag.

He shoves his pad farther into his backpack, zips it closed, hands me the half-filled-in sheet, and walks back to his desk.

***

I'm eating my burger with extra pickles when Ava squeezes in next to me with her lunch tray. "Well, how are your magical powers today? Turned Izzie into a frog or a lizard?"

"Why a frog or a lizard?"

"Really? That's what you're focused on?" Ava says. "Not the part where you have the power to magically transform your foster sister into a reptile?" She laughs.

I lean my head on my best friend's shoulder. "She's my sister for only a few more days. Then she's my"—I don't know what to say—"nothing. I guess."

"Maybe you can harness your magical powers and change that. Again." She smiles and takes a bite of her peanut-butter-and-marshmallow-fluff sandwich.

"If I had powers, I'd get my parents to keep her." *And my mom to stay out of my stuff.* I keep that wish to myself and the universe.

"If I had powers, I'd be a famous coder," Ava says, "and I wouldn't have to share a bathroom with my brothers who leave the toilet seat up."

"If I had powers, I'd want my sister not to be great at every single thing she does," Sam says, joining us and dunking her fries into ketchup.

As Ava and Sam continue talking about magic, I guzzle the last of my milk and slide the empty container into my backpack.

"What are you doing with that?" Ava wants to know.

"With what?" Sam asks.

Ava points to the empty milk carton. "That garbage. Why are you saving it?"

All eyes stare at me. My secret feels like it might spill out and stick to the table like old ketchup.

But then I laugh, like of course I'm not saving trash. "It's for Charlie, for this project he wants us to do together." I hold my breath and hope that sounds like a thing I would do.

"Oh. Want mine, too?" Ava asks. She finishes her milk and hands me her empty carton.

"Thanks," I say.

When I look up, Mason's staring at me from across the cafeteria.

Slowly, I zip the milk cartons into my bag.

21

The Girl with the Sparkly Headband

When I get home, I step over Charlie's Lego castle and head to my room. Thankfully, it looks like Mom hasn't been back in here since our run-in this morning. My bed and floor and desk are still littered with stuff. I move the *Guinness World Records* book that Charlie and I checked out from the library and dig out a box from underneath my bed. I survey my memories and drop in the milk cartons from lunch. I sit with my stuff for a while. Wrapped in a kind of peacefulness. Then I clean my room enough so Mom doesn't come in and do it with me.

Or *for* me.

That's when I hear crying. First, I think it's Izzie,

but then realize it's Charlie. When I open the door to my bedroom, Charlie's sitting just outside. His eyes are red, his cheeks are wet, and there's a trail of snot running from his nose.

I hand him a tissue. "What's wrong, Bear?"

"Emma Rose. She wouldn't let me play four square again. I told her I was a fast learner, just like you said, but it didn't work." He ignores the tissue and uses his sleeve instead.

I hold my little brother's hand. "I have an idea."

His big, round eyes look in mine.

"Do you trust me?" I ask.

He nods.

"Okay. Let's do this."

I tell Mom the plan, recruit Dillon, grab chalk and a red rubber ball, and we walk with Charlie back to the school playground. The three of us. The sun's shining bright, so it's packed with kids. To the left is a pickup basketball game. Dillon glances over at me.

"Later," I say. "Now we need you to help make a new four-square champion."

I look at Charlie. When he smiles, I can see the

hole from the tooth he lost last week. He bit into a crunchy McIntosh, and his tooth stuck. Right to the core of the apple.

We pass kids laughing on the tire swing, climbing the monkey bars, and jumping off the swings. But Charlie's smile disappears as we get to the edge of the blacktop. Three girls are huddled together talking, and just behind them is a line of kids waiting to play four square. Emma Rose is serving. As we get closer to the bouncing ball, Charlie tugs my shirt. "Let's come back later. When it's empty."

"You've got this," I whisper to my little brother. "I promise. We're right here with you." His mouth twists in a way that says he's not totally convinced.

Emma Rose pushes back her sparkly headband and holds the ball. She glances over and puts her hands on her hips. Instead of getting in line to play *that* game, Dillon draws a new four-square box. Then he hands Charlie the ball. Charlie looks at me, and I nod. He says in the smallest of whispers, "Anyone want to play?"

I step into one square. Dillon steps in another.

No one else moves.

Charlie bites his lip, which is now in full quiver mode.

Okay, Universe, help my little brother out. He just needs one kid. One kid to say yes.

Emma Rose serves, and the boy in the box misses. Emma Rose makes a not-so-nice face.

Another boy moves out of line and steps into the last empty box of Charlie's four squares.

Thank you, Universe.

"Hi, I'm Charlie." He hands the boy the ball. "You can serve."

The boy smiles. "Thanks. My name's Aarush."

Dillon gets out first. Then me. And with each out, another kid slides into Charlie's game. Where no one is making a not-so-nice face.

Soon, only Emma Rose is standing in her four squares.

Charlie looks at me and then at Emma Rose.

"Want to play?" he asks the girl wearing the sparkly headband.

She nods and steps into one of Charlie's four squares.

22

Not Garbage!

It's been five days since Hurricane Berma hit Louisiana. Ms. López is organizing a book drive to send new and gently loved books to the schools that flooded. Dad's rebroadcasting our *How to Find Your Pet After a Natural Disaster* episode. And the adoptive couple is working on the fastest way to get out of Louisiana. Mom said a levee broke, there are major power outages, lots of road closures, and the airport is running only humanitarian efforts. Which means no flights out for Maya and Asher.

With each day Izzie stays with us, I love her more. That's the second weird thing I've learned about love. The first is that it smells like powder. The second is that it grows. Even if you don't water it. Which is different from everything in Nana's garden.

"Can I come in?" It's Mom.

She sits next to me on my bed before I can answer. Then she reaches for my hand. "We need to talk."

"I put lots of my stuff away," I say, looking around at my mostly neater room.

She nods. "Thank you."

I let go of her hand and slide down under my daisy-yellow comforter. "Was there another hurricane?" I cross my fingers and silently tell the universe there can't be any more horrible storms.

"No hurricane," she says.

I uncross my fingers.

"When I took Izzie on a walk today, I couldn't find her yellow sock or her frog binkie." She sighs. "I looked all over the house. Finally, I found them both under your bed. On the floor." I scoot farther away from my mom, no longer wondering where Charlie gets his best-finder gene.

A tornadolike anger spins through my body. "You

agreed not to go into my stuff!" I get out of my bed. "And they weren't on the floor. They were in a box!" A burning hot spreads across my face and chest.

Her voice is calm. "Maybe they *were* in a box, but today they were on the floor. With—"

"They were not on the floor! They were in one of my private you-can't-touch boxes!" My lungs feel like they're squeezing all the air out of me.

"Maggie, I wasn't trying to invade your space. I was looking for Isabelle's things. Nothing more."

"You had no right going into my stuff!" I yell from my angry place.

I flip up my comforter and look under my bed. There's Izzie's sock, a sliver of diaper tape, strands of baby hair, two napkins, five gum wrappers, the gecko necklace, the tassel from Nana's scarf, the milk cartons, the binkie, the button, the rocks, the blanket threads, the butterscotch candy wrappers, the photos, and the three bendy straws. Some of these things are in my boxes. Some are on the floor. I don't remember anything being on the floor.

"What did you do?" I ask my mother. The words dart out, sharp and accusing.

"Nothing. This was how I found your things. Spilled like garbage."

"They're not garbage!"

"Of course they're garbage! There are empty milk cartons with ants in them." She picks up a carton with a line of ants marching along the rim.

"You don't understand! You don't get it! You don't get *me*," I scream as anger rips through my body.

In that moment, I'm thankful no one else is home to hear my voice bounce off the walls. "Did you take anything?"

She shakes her head no, her brown curls moving with her. But I don't believe her. I pull out my boxes from under my bed and survey my stuff. Then I move to the closet and do the same thing. When I'm done, I'm sitting in a sea of cardboard. I exhale. An ant crawls over my foot.

She tries again. "Honey, what is all this stuff? Why do you have pieces of random things dumped all over the floor? Why are you keeping empty containers and old clothes and trash?" She moves toward me.

Don't.

"It's not trash! It's my stuff. I need it."

She points to the ants on my floor.

Were they here before?

Then she picks up the used yellow plastic fork and the half of a red, white, and blue plate with fireworks on it from our family's Fourth of July picnic last year. "What could you possibly need these for?" Her arms stretch out to her sides, her worried eyebrows letting me know she doesn't understand.

"To remember." My voice is so low it's even hard for me to hear.

"And this?" She's holding an empty gum wrapper from our first trap practice as an all-girl squad.

"Let go of my stuff!" I yell.

"Don't raise your voice to me, Maggie. We've talked about that. I'm trying to figure out what's going on." She drops the wrapper.

"I keep it to remember." *How doesn't she get that?*

I grab my wrapper and tuck it into the top of one of the boxes.

"Remember what?" Her arms fall to her sides. Concern and confusion worm into the wrinkles around her eyes.

"Trap practice, my great presentation on Punnett squares, the day with Gramps at Box Mart, the hikes up Ridge Mountain, the lunches with my friends, Izzie, Nana."

Everything freezes when I mention Nana. I see the pain flash in Mom's eyes. I know it. I feel it. It's the pain I get every time I think I'm going to forget.

Something.

Everything.

"You don't need these things to remember," Mom says.

"Yes, I do!"

"No, you don't. This is garbage and threads and pieces of random things."

I shake my head. Back and forth and back and forth and back and forth. There are no words for how wrong she is.

But she doesn't stop. In a gentle voice, she says, "Memories stay with you. In your heart."

"Then why do you keep Nana's charm bracelet?" I ask in a not-so-gentle voice. Ever since Nana died, Mom's had that gold chain wrapped around her wrist.

"That's different."

"No, it's not. You wear that bracelet so you don't forget Nana the way she forgot you."

She rests her hand over the heart charm. "Maggie." Another step toward me. "I wear this bracelet to feel close to Nana, not because I'm worried I'll forget her. I could never forget her. That's how love works. And the only reason Nana forgot anything was because she had dementia. I don't have that, and neither do you."

I stop listening, slam close the lids of my boxes, and stand in front of them. "There's no garbage in here. And we're not touching or cleaning or throwing out anything!" My voice gets louder with every syllable. "So leave my stuff alone! And get out of my room!"

"Maggie, let's talk."

"You don't understand!" I'm screaming. Again.

"We need to clean out these boxes and the stuff under your bed. Get rid of the ants and the garbage," she says. "We can do it together."

"No! I hate you! You're the worst mom ever!" The words crash and anchor between us. "I won't let you take away my sister *and* my memories!"

Then it happens.

The anger drapes across my brain and digs like nails into my heart. I take the plate, plastic fork, shirt, perfume bottle, bath mat, and throw them at my mother, one by one.

23

Drift and Drain

Mom puts her hands in front of her face and, in a very loud voice, says, "Don't!" as she storms out of my room. I know she's gone. Not for good. But for now. Space. That's her thing. She needs it. "Never talk from the place where anger lives." That's what she always says. "You have to give those feelings room to drift and drain."

I drag my daisy-yellow comforter and my double stack of pillows onto the floor in front of my bedroom door, like the Queen's Guard in front of Buckingham Palace. No one's coming in my room, plucking my things, and tossing them into the garbage. No one!

They are not trash.

They are not junk.

They are not nothing.

They are mine. To keep. Forever.

Batman snuggles next to my body. I hug him tight and know, in the place that holds my truth, that he understands. That he loves me. No matter what.

I hear Bert moving around in his tub. His home. I open my Go On, Change the World! notebook, grab my purple pen, and write:

1. *Never forget.*
2. *Don't let go.*

I flip to a clean sheet and start a sketch of Nana from the photo she took the day I showed her how to take a selfie. She's standing in front of her tomato plants, laughing, happiness splashed across her face. While I draw, I listen to "Up on the Roof" by Carole King. I love Carole King and this song. My boxes are like her roof. My safe place. To hide.

Mom doesn't understand. She doesn't even like Carole King. She didn't get the music gene. I got that from Dad and Gramps. Ava says I have an old person DJing from inside myself.

Somewhere between lyrics, my anger slides, and in its place is a huge helping of you're-the-worst-daughter-ever.

I step into my orange slippers and tiptoe downstairs. Mom's drinking tea and reading in the big brown oversized chair. She lifts her head and pats the space next to her. Her warmness feels undeserved. "I'm sorry," I say.

"I know." She takes my hand in hers and draws my chin up so I'm looking right into her deep-green eyes. "But what you did can never happen again. There is no time that throwing things and yelling are ever okay." Her voice is strong, resolute, unwavering.

I nod.

"What was that about?" She takes a sip of her tea.

"Not sure. All I know is that it felt bad and I couldn't make it stop."

"Make *what* stop?"

"The most mad ever. It was huge. Like it should have a different name."

"What made you so angry?"

"You touching my stuff." It was like those other times, when she wanted to clean my room and Charlie tried to get his ball from under my bed. But worse. Way worse.

"Why?"

I shrug, because I honestly don't know.

We sit like this for a while.

"It's going to be okay," she says as I lean against her.

I start to cry and she wipes my tears. "Dad and I will figure out the best way to help you. The best way to make the mad go away. Together." Then she kisses my forehead.

I'm not sure how they can help. *If* they can help. But for now, I'm relieved my angry feelings have seeped out.

I hug my mom and go upstairs. I peek into Charlie's room. He looks up from his parade of animals. "Did you know that turtles can breathe through their butts?"

I love my little brother.

24

A Mound of Scared

I turn off my alarm and wrap my comforter around my tired body. Batman snuggles close, and I hear Bert swimming in his tub. My room feels safe. Like in here, under my covers, nothing bad can happen.

Mom finds me in bed when I don't come down for pancakes. "Are you sick?" she asks as she touches my forehead to see if I'm running a fever.

I'm not sick. Or running a fever. But I don't say anything. I don't want to lie. I also don't want to go to school or talk about what happened last night. And I especially don't want my mad to spill out. Again.

She leans in and kisses my head. "It's going to be okay. I left a message for Dr. Felger."

The last time I saw my pediatrician I had strep throat. She gave me medicine, and in two days I felt totally normal. I wonder if there's magic medicine that will make my ugly feelings go away. "Can I stay home from school today?" I ask my mom.

Her head tilts slightly to the right as she brushes the hair out of my eyes. "Your Gimme Day?"

I nod. It's a day I get to stay home even if I'm not fever-or-vomit-sick. Dillon, Charlie, and I each get one a school year. Charlie never takes his. Dillon always asks for extra.

"Do you think Dr. Felger is going to need to see me?" The thought of visiting my pediatrician's office today doesn't feel like a real Gimme Day.

"I'm not sure. Let's see what she says."

Mom leaves my room, and I fall back to sleep until Batman licks my face and wakes me. I slide out of bed and onto my floor, reach into one of my boxes, and touch Izzie's little yellow sock. I rub Batman's belly, happy we're his forever family. Then I make a sign for my boxes:

PLEASE DO NOT TOUCH MY STUFF. DO NOT THROW OUT ANYTHING. THANK YOU. MAGGIE.

I might not understand the anger, but when I think about anyone moving or touching my things, it's there. Stuck to me like sap.

I walk into the hall, close my bedroom door, and go find Izzie. She's in the kitchen with Mom, who hands me a plate of pancakes and sits in the seat next to mine. "Let's talk about what happened last night."

I swallow hard.

"Why do you think you got so angry when I touched your stuff?"

She waits for me to answer. To explain. But I don't. I can't.

I shake my head. "Mom, not now." The silence stretches across the kitchen table. "Please."

She lays her soft hands on top of mine. "Okay, for now." She sighs loudly. "We'll wait and see what Dr. Felger suggests."

When I finish my breakfast, I leave to visit

Gramps. Being with him always makes everything feel less bad and less scary and less confusing. Not sure why. Maybe it's the garden. Or the reminders of Nana everywhere.

When I get there, Gramps is sitting in Nana's chair on the screened-in porch, watching the cardinals and robins at the bird feeder. This month's *Celebrity Life* is open on his lap. It was Nana's subscription. Every month for the last year, he has sat in her chair and read all the pop gossip. I tell him I'm taking my Gimme Day, settle into *his* chair, and sketch his face. His nose is a little crooked. Left over from when he broke it playing hockey as a kid. Neither one of us says anything. We watch the birds and read and draw.

He hands me two bowls. One filled with yellow tomatoes and the other filled with prunes. I take a handful of the tomatoes.

"Want to talk about it?" he asks after a long while. Nana used to say Gramps had some kind of extrasensory perception. Like he just knew things. Lots of things. Kind of like Charlie, but less random.

"Not sure," I say. Because in the place that keeps my secrets, I don't think I'm ready to let the words go.

"Then we can just sit. Nana used to say sitting helps."

So we sit.

And sit.

And sit.

It kind of helps.

"This thing happened with Mom," I say. "She did something that made me mad."

I don't tell him the mad was so big it felt like it swallowed my whole body. Or that it was followed by a mound of scared. And throwing things.

"Hmm."

"I'm fine, though." Not sure I totally believe that. "Everyone saves stuff," I tell him, popping a tomato in my mouth.

He nods.

"I think it's way weirder that Charlie collects random facts. I mean, who needs to know that for every one person there are a million ants?"

Gramps gets up, and when he comes back, he hands me a small glass jar.

It's filled with six dried flowers.

"What are these?" I ask.

"They're flowers from mine and Nana's wedding, and our tenth, twentieth, thirtieth, fortieth, and fiftieth wedding anniversaries."

"Why?"

"Don't know really. Nana saved them. She said they made her happy."

"Maybe she kept them so she wouldn't forget."

"That's the thing, Maggie." He turns to face me. "These things *didn't* keep her from forgetting." He stops as tears fill around his crystal-blue eyes. "Sometimes people *do* forget. Either because they're sick, like Nana, or they're just too little to remember, like Izzie. Truth is, life's filled with give and take. Details fade. Or even erase entirely. But love never leaves. It carves into your heart. It's a forever thing."

25

A Plan

My Gimme Day is over, and my parents tell me I can't stay home again.

They also tell me there's a plan.

Dr. Felger wants me to see a psychologist. For kids.

Today.

After school.

I try not to think about it as I head to art, my last class of the day. Honestly, I haven't wanted to think about it since Mom and Dad told me last night. They came into my room with their serious faces. Then Mom told me about her conversation with Dr. Felger, who's known me since I fell on the ice and needed stitches in my chin when I was four.

"I know this is not what you expected," Mom said.

"I thought maybe *she'd* want to see me. Not send me off to some stranger therapist person."

"I get that," Dad said, reaching for my hand. "But this is someone Dr. Felger trusts and believes is in the best position to help."

"You said that *we'd* fix this." I pulled my hand away.

"And we will," he said. "But we can't do it alone. We need guidance. Information. Resources. So we can fix it. Together."

As I grab my seat at the art table, I wonder when "together" started including a complete stranger. I look around the room. Mason's across from me. We're working on portraits. His looks like the face of a woman. Mine's of Izzie.

Mr. Rodriguez comes over to our table. His head is bald, his beard is midnight black, and he's wearing a T-shirt that says PAINT ON. "I really like how you've drawn the baby's eyes," he says.

"Thanks."

"What's her name?"

"Izzie," I say like she's family.

"She kind of looks like you."

A jolt of happiness zips through me.

He walks over to Mason, looks at his sketch, and says something I can't hear. Mason looks down and nods, and Mr. Rodriguez pats his back. I'm about to ask if he's okay when Mason gets up and walks out of the art room.

At the end of the school day, I look for Mason but don't find him at his locker. Maybe he's taking a Gimme Afternoon. I grab my backpack and am relieved Ava had to leave early to get her braces fixed. I haven't told her about the mad or the boxes or the doctor. Part of me wants to tell her everything. But the other part doesn't want to risk it. No one wants to be friends with someone who does weird stuff.

Before I can decide which part will win, I spy Mom and Dad waiting for me outside of school, and a big fat knot worms into my stomach.

I get into our truck, kiss a sleeping Izzie, and stare out the window until we pull into the parking lot of an unfamiliar building with a sign that says

THE SPARROW CENTER, DR. MARGARET SPARROW,
CLINICAL PSYCHOLOGIST.

The plan.

Begins.

Now.

26

Meatball Sub

When Dad turns off the engine, my body freezes.

I'm scared.

Scared of the mad. Scared of the doctor. Scared of all the what-ifs.

"I don't want to do this," I say. "It's dumb."

"It's not dumb, Maggie. It's important," Mom says.

Dad opens my door. "I know it's hard, but it's going to be okay."

"You don't know that." My feelings spin.

I look at my parents. And their serious, worried faces. I know there's no way they're letting me stay in this truck. I uncross my arms, undo my seat belt, and open the door.

Dr. Sparrow's office smells like a meatball sub. Izzie doesn't seem to notice—she's sound asleep in her car seat. But my stomach rumbles. Lunch was hours ago. And I shared half of my peanut-butter-and-fluff sandwich with Ava. I also had one milk. Which left me with one empty carton to save for later.

I'm sitting between Mom and Dad. Mom's tapping her foot and playing solitaire on her phone. Dad's humming, like this is just another afternoon together at Big Al's Diner eating turkey-and-potato-chip sandwiches. Like I'm not scared. Or embarrassed. To talk about my box or the fight or the ugly mad.

There's a boy across the room with a Celtics cap and curly blond hair. I wonder if his parents and pediatrician made him come, too. The front door opens, and a girl with a long, shiny dark braid walks in. Her shirt sparkles. She sees me and gives me a weak smile. A man with a mess of hair and a blazer comes in with her, says something to the person at the front desk, and leaves quickly, with the promise to return soon. Her weak smile turns into something less happy.

I walk over and offer her a piece of grape gum. She takes the gum and pops it into her mouth.

"Mr. and Mrs. Hunt and Maggie, you guys can come back now," says a woman with blue hair.

I leave the waiting room and follow the woman, my parents, and Baby Izzie into Dr. Sparrow's office.

When we get there, Dr. Sparrow steps out from behind her desk. She reminds me of Nana, with her strong handshake and red lipstick. Except Nana would never wear a bright-pink sweater.

Then Dr. Sparrow explains how this will work—first she'll have a conversation alone with Mom and Dad, then I'll rejoin the group.

"Do you have any questions?" Dr. Sparrow asks me.

"No," I say. Which isn't entirely true, but my brain is flooded with loud bursts of I-don't-want-to-be-here, so I'm not sure I can even form actual sentences.

I move to another waiting room. It's empty of people, but the wall is filled with one big quote: THE GREAT THING IN THIS WORLD IS NOT SO MUCH WHERE WE STAND, AS IN WHAT DIRECTION WE ARE MOVING. —OLIVER WENDELL HOLMES

I read it twice, then decide I don't get it and open my phone to play Litmus. I need to answer three questions in this category correctly to pass the litmus test and move to the next level. The questions are: (1) What's the name of the town where guitarist Lucy Billings was raised? (2) Where did rocker Mack Bates attend music school? and (3) What instrument did Lila Lu play before taking up piano at the age of twenty-two? I get them all right. Number two is a trick question. Mack Bates never even went to school for music. He majored in business and played guitar to make some money. After jamming for a year, he quit school and moved to Nashville.

I'm about to move on to level two when I'm called back into the doctor's office.

Mom and Dad smile at me. I don't smile back.

Dr. Sparrow rolls her chair from behind the desk so that she's sitting across from me.

I notice a framed photo of a chubby baby in a onesie that says MY AUNTIE ROCKS.

"Who's the baby?" I ask.

"Maggie, that's not really why we're here," Mom says.

And why exactly are we here? Because you think I collect garbage or because I freaked out when you tried to throw it away?

"That's okay," Dr. Sparrow says. "That's my new niece, Lacey."

I want to ask if she's temporary, but I don't.

"Your parents shared that your family is taking care of a foster baby." She points to the tiny human sleeping in the car seat next to Mom.

"Her name's Izzie. Isn't she supercute?" I say, peeling the mint-green nail polish off my right pointer finger.

Dr. Sparrow's smile is real—and lovely except for the speck of meatball wedged between her front teeth. I wonder if I sweep my tongue across my teeth she'll get the urge to do the same. But I glance over at Mom and already know that falls outside any reason we're here.

"Before we continue, Maggie, I want to know if you'd like to talk with me alone or with your parents here."

A tiny drop of me doesn't want to be this scared without them, but the rest of me needs space. To talk. About all of it. "I think I want to do this myself." I pause. "For now."

My parents get up, love and worry woven into their faces.

"If you need us, we'll just be in the waiting room," Dad says as he closes the door behind him.

Dr. Sparrow asks me about school, Izzie, and trap. All the easy stuff. Then she sits back and says, "Tell me about the boxes under your bed."

27

Boxes Under My Bed

"I'm not sure what my parents told you, but my boxes are just a place to keep my stuff."

Sort of true.

"They're actually no big deal."

Not really true. I freak out when anyone goes near my things. I pop a piece of gum in my mouth.

"Can you tell me what kind of things you save?"

I wonder if she saw me keep the wrapper.

"Three milk cartons, five gum wrappers, three bendy straws, six rocks, three sticks, two napkins, one baby sock, tabs from two diapers, a small piece from a disposable bottle, wisps of Izzie's hair, threads from a baby blanket, one frog binkie, a button from Bud the Bear, one gecko necklace, one scarf tassel, one yellow plastic fork, one fireworks paper plate, two butterscotch candy wrappers, and all the photos I've taken of Izzie." I pause. "That's what's in my newest box."

"How many boxes do you have?"

My mouth twists as the truth slips out. "Seven in my closet. Four under my bed. And, um." I stop there.

"And what?" she asks.

I stare at the floor. "I keep things in my locker at school, too." Tears roll down my cheeks.

She slides a tissue box closer to me.

"I really don't want to do this," I say.

"Do what?"

"Talk about any of this stuff."

"I know," she says. "It can feel hard. We don't have to discuss everything all at once."

We talk for a while about Nana and Izzie. Then she asks me, "Why do you keep these things?"

"Why does anyone keep anything? To remember. The walk, the lunch, the game, the museum, my nana, my baby, um, my Izzie."

Dr. Sparrow leans toward me. "Maggie, you don't need to save stuff to hold on to those memories. I promise that your heart and brain will remember the things that are important to you."

"Nana's didn't," I say. Then I tell her all about Forgot-Me Day.

"That must have been very hard," she says. "And painful for you. But your parents told me that Nana's forgetfulness was from dementia. That's very different. Your grandmother's brain had a disease that made it difficult to remember. You don't have that. You're a healthy twelve-year-old with a healthy brain."

I pause and stare at the floor to find my brave. I inhale the smell of meatball sub and say, "Then what's wrong with me? What made my anger so big I didn't know it could even fit inside my body?"

Before she answers, she peppers me with lots more questions about my stuff and my worries. She wants to know how long I've been saving. The first thing I put in my box. What my worry feels like when I think I may forget. Or when I think someone may throw something out. When I'm done

146

answering, my mouth is dry and I have no more secrets.

"Maggie, I believe you have anxiety," Dr. Sparrow says. "Many kids worry about all different kinds of things. Some are afraid of swimming or the dark or dogs. You're afraid of forgetting." She slides her chair closer to me. "Anxiety can be hereditary. Like height and freckles and red hair."

"Who did I get it from?"

"Your mom shared that she worried a lot when she was a kid, even though she was never diagnosed. And she said your cousin Alec wrestles with anxiety, too."

I remember Alec worrying about spiders and the poodle who lived next door the last time we visited him. "But why would anxiety about forgetting make me so mad?"

"The things you collect are tied to specific memories. And when you think someone might move or toss those items, you worry that the very memories associated with those things will vanish as well. And that worry makes you angry."

"Wait! You think I'm like the people who can't

throw stuff away on those hoarding shows? The people who live between stacks of stuff? I'm not like them! My room isn't full of lamps and mail and garbage." My palms are wet with sweat.

Dr. Sparrow shakes her head. "I don't think you're like the adults on those shows. Hoarding in adults is often different than hoarding in kids. It can look different and be done for different reasons. But you do have a personal attachment to a lot of items that many may not consider worth saving. And you have anxiety and anger around letting go of those things."

"So you do think I hoard, just not like a grown-up?"

"The label isn't really helpful. Especially with the popularity of those shows. What is helpful is understanding that lots of kids worry. And your worry is tied to letting go. So that's what we're going to work on."

My head nods, but my brain sticks on the idea that I'm a hoarder. A kid hoarder.

"The first thing I'm going to ask you to do is to give your worry a name," Dr. Sparrow says.

"Like a person or a pet?" I ask.

"Exactly," she says.

"That's weird."

She smiles. "Maybe. But I want you to name it, and when you feel the worry bubble up inside, you're going to tell it to go away."

"Then what?"

"Move on to something else. Your mom and dad told me that you love music and drawing. Doing those things will help you reroute your thoughts and keep your mind off the anxiety."

I lean back in my chair. "If everyone with a healthy brain can remember everything they need in their head and heart, why are there scrapbooks and photo albums?"

"Some things are okay to save. And a scrapbook and photo album are healthy ways to do that."

"So are boxes under your bed and in your closet," I say.

"For some things, that may be okay, and for others, it may not. Let's talk about how to tell the difference."

We talk for a while about things to keep and

things to toss. The okay things to keep: photos and photo albums and a gecko necklace from your nana. The not-okay things to keep: wrappers and used paper plates, sticks and rocks, old toothbrushes and bath mats, broken hairbrushes, and clothes that don't fit. Mostly everything in my boxes falls into the not-okay-to-save category.

Then Dr. Sparrow tells me it's going to be all right.

I'm going to be all right.

We can fix this.

Together.

I'm just not sure I believe her.

28

The Hole in My Heart

All night, I think about what to name my worry. Fred. Ralph. Jax. None of those feel right. Rae. Mac. Lucy. None of those work, either. I'm starting to wonder if I'll even know when I find the right name. I lie on my back and listen to the rain and thunder outside. I wish I could call Ava and ask her what she thinks would be a good name for my worry. But I know I can't. No sharing. Except with Batman and Bert. And Mom and Dad. They know. They always know. I can't hide from them. Even if I wanted to.

I wonder about Dillon and Charlie. Charlie saw my ugly mad but doesn't know the rest. And Dillon's gone so much with basketball, I don't think he's even noticed. It doesn't matter now. My stuff is safe. No one's allowed to touch anything. Doctor's orders.

I roll over, and the word *cipher* flashes across my brain. I remember it because I got the definition wrong on Litmus last week. I didn't know what it meant. Dad said a cipher is a type of puzzle. An enigma. Like my anxiety, and how it makes me hold on to things. Something I don't understand. I ask Batman if he thinks the word fits, and he licks my ear.

"Okay, Cipher, that's your name. Now leave me alone!" I say to my worry. Then I listen to "Calling All Angels" by Train as I drift off to sleep.

On Monday at school, I'm quiet and keep to myself. Ava and Gracie and Sam ask if I'm okay. I tell them I think I might be getting sick. Truth is, I want to hide under my covers until my scary mad disappears forever. But my Gimme Day is used up, and when I get home, Charlie's waiting for me. He wants to play. I don't, but his brown eyes beg me to be the kind of big sister he needs.

I look outside and have an idea. I put Bert in his carrier and head out back with Charlie. His job: be sure Bert stays in his carrier on the lawn. My job:

find the baby pool. Mom put it somewhere in the outgrown-it section of the garage with the boxes of our too-small clothes, the red tricycles, and the mini scooters she plans to sell at her annual Get-Rid-of-It Yard Sale. The yard sale where I secretly reclaim my stuff and put it in my boxes.

I find the blue pool with the pictures of ducks on it leaning against the wall behind the baby floaties, plastic shovels, and stackable buckets. Charlie smiles when he sees me dragging it across the lawn. I flop it down, grab the hose, spray off the left-behind dirt, and fill it with water. We open the turtle carrier and put Bert and a few rocks in the pool. The sun hits the water as he swims around. After a few laps, he finds the rock and basks.

"Did you know the world's oldest living tortoise is named Jonathan?" Charlie says, digging up a few worms. He gives one to Batman—who smells it, ignores it, and runs after something under the bushes—and then puts the rest in the pool for Bert.

"I didn't."

"Did you know he got his first bath at 184?"

"Nope," I say. "Glad you didn't wait that long."

Charlie laughs. "Me too. I'd be stinky, like a bombardier beetle."

I stare at my little brother, wondering how he got the random-knowledge gene and I got the one filled with anxiety.

When the sun moves behind the clouds, Charlie, Bert, and I head inside. Batman stays in the yard, in search of the thing under the bushes.

I find Izzie in her bassinet, grab Shel Silverstein's *Where the Sidewalk Ends*, and read her my favorite poem, "Hug o' War." Mom comes in on the last line: "And everyone wins." She smiles.

"You've always loved that book," she says, then kisses the top of my head. "I just heard from Rita. Izzie will be heading to her new family soon."

"When's soon?"

"I don't have a specific date yet."

My insides dip.

I should be happy.

But I'm not.

Mom sits down next to me and shows me a page she has open on her computer. At the top it says:

Meet Maya and Asher.

"This is the couple who's adopting Izzie," Mom says. "I thought you'd want to know more about them." She takes Izzie, and I take the computer. I read all about the new family our baby is going to be a part of.

About us:
We met during our first year of law school. Immediately, we knew there was something special, and got married soon after graduation. We run a nonprofit organization that helps protect children from unsafe products.

Qualities we see in each other:
Asher believes that Maya is the kindest person he knows. She is thoughtful, dedicated, intelligent, and hardworking in everything she does.
Maya believes that Asher is loving, smart, and considerate.

Hobbies:
We enjoy reading, travel, hiking, biking, puzzles, and time with family. We also love time spent at home watching old movies. We can't wait to include our new

baby in our life. We hope to get a puppy and watch them grow up together.

Our extended family:

Maya has two brothers who live in Louisiana, and they each have three boys. Asher's sister and parents live nearby. Happily, our home is often filled with extended family. So there will be lots of cousins and family to love and welcome our new baby.

Our home and neighborhood:

Our home is warm and sunny. It has a fenced-in back-yard, and we recently started a small vegetable garden. The town we live in has one of the best school districts in the state. It is a perfect place to raise a child. We look forward to raising our family here.

They sound like good people. Kind people. People who don't have worries they need to name. People who will love Izzie.

But that doesn't fill the bottomless hole in my heart.

29

Like Dominoes

All I want now is to be close to Izzie. I'm scared of forgetting her. Even if I believe Dr. Sparrow and do everything she says. Even if I tell Cipher to go away. I still worry if I forget one memory, the rest will leak out.

That's what happened with Nana. I know Dr. Sparrow says that's different. That I'm not like Nana. But what if she's wrong? What if that's just how memories work? What if they're like dominoes? One memory falls. Then another. And another. Until there are none left.

I grab my favorite pen—and my Go On, Change

the World! notebook, and open to a blank page. In big letters I write:

> *Don't forget*
> *what you love.*
> *Don't forget*
> *who you love.*
> *Don't forget*
> *anything.*
> *Ever.*

I tuck the book back into my desk. I hear Dad recording a new episode in the linen closet. Something about garbage. Lots of garbage. Reusing it and turning it into electricity. Charlie will love this.

I look over at Izzie. When her bright eyes pop open, I gently pick her up, and we walk to the kitchen to get her a bottle. The light above the sink hums. Mom offers to take my little bean, but I don't want to let her go. Not yet. We sit on the overstuffed couch with the beat of the day playing around us. The birds chirp, and the squirrels chase one another up the tree in the backyard. I lean back and give Izzie her bottle. She slurps and sucks until there's nothing left. I kiss her soft cheek and beg Mom to let me stay home from school today. So I can be close. To my sister.

Mom answers with a nonnegotiable no and takes our little human from me.

As the shower water sprays my hair, I think of Izzie and saying good-bye. I think of the things in my boxes that I have to toss. I know that Cipher will be mad to see them go. A chill worms into the warm water.

When I'm done, Dad's waiting for me in the car. The ride to school is filled with talk about his new podcasts. "So what do you think about reusable trash?" he says.

"Who wouldn't love someone else's used, dirty stuff?" I say.

"Maggie, it's amazing. Businesses are turning garbage into renewable energy. Isn't that cool?"

I nod. His excitement is too big to disagree with.

"What do you think about cloning?" he asks.

"I'm a fan," I say. No one would ever be forever gone.

Then there's a long awkward pause, the kind where the silence feels loud. "Maggie, I know you're going through a hard time. I'm not the best at this kind of thing, but I want you to know I'm proud of you."

"Thanks, Dad."

"I'm here if you want to talk."

"I know."

He nods and gives my hand a squeeze.

School feels like I'm sleepwalking. I'm here, but not really. I spend most of English not listening to Ms. López and much of geometry yelling at Cipher in my head.

When Dad picks me up after school for trap practice, my brain is full of worry. I let him talk. He's excited about some new technology that can sniff out disease. As we pull into the parking lot of Fish, Fur, and Fly, I'm starting to understand where Charlie gets his love of random information.

The colored leaves crunch under my feet as I

walk to the squad meeting spot. I love the red ones best. They look like fire and my hair and the ripest tomatoes in Gramps's garden.

I see Ava, Sam, and Gracie over by the hot cider and doughnuts. I splash on a fake smile and make sure the part of me that's tied to my stuff and my doctor is hidden.

Dad calls everyone over. He runs down the safety rules and the list of additional practices and who's attended. I'm surprised that Sam's been to the last three of the four additional practices even though she already has the six needed to qualify for the state tournament.

"Where's Mason?" Dad asks the squad, like that's a question we'd know the answer to.

"I bet he quit," Ava says.

"More doughnuts for me!" Gracie adds, holding a Boston cream in one hand and a chocolate glazed in the other.

"He can't leave now. We need him to win," Sam says, tugging on her Red Sox cap.

I take my spot at position one. But when I look down the line, my insides sink when I see the gap where Belle used to be. A hole in our squad. "If Mason quit, Belle can return," I tell Dad. "You know, we can go back to the way things were. The Original Five."

"I bet he couldn't handle all the girl power," Gracie says, pulling up her lucky purple socks.

Ava shoots, shattering a clay disc into tiny pieces. "Let's face it. He's a quitter," she says.

"Missing one practice doesn't mean he quit," Dad says. "Maybe he's sick. Or had a dentist appointment or a haircut or had some other ordinary reason for missing practice. For now, let's just focus on the clay pigeons."

But I can't. I hear Mason's dad's voice in my head saying we're not the best group of anything, and wonder if our team is truly broken.

30

They're Me

Mom reads her students' college essays in the waiting room while I meet with Dr. Sparrow. It's been five days since I first walked into the office that smelled like meatball sub. Today, Dr. Sparrow's wearing a bright-blue shirt with yellow stars. She pulls her chair out from behind her desk and sits across from me. I stare at her and decide I still don't want to be here.

She explains that I need to list the items in my boxes and my locker, and rate them from zero to ten on a chart. Zero is something that's easy to toss in the garbage, and ten is the stuff that feels impossible to throw away. "And each time you toss something, you get reward points," she says. "The harder an item is to let go, the more points you'll earn."

She smiles when she talks, as if this will somehow make me like being here more. Or make throwing my stuff away easier. "What am I supposed to do with a bunch of points?" I ask, wondering if she earned her shirt on the point system.

"The points accrue, and when you reach different milestone markers, like thirty-five, fifty, and a hundred points, you get a prize. You and your parents can decide what markers make the most sense, given the number of items you need to toss and how difficult it is to let go of them."

"What kind of prize?"

"Often patients use them for something special they want to buy or something fun they want to do. It depends what matters most to you."

I think of all the things in my boxes and my locker that matter. That I don't want to let go. Dr. Sparrow says this is one step toward getting rid of the ugly mad that's attached to all my stuff.

"I don't want to do this," I say, my voice cracking. "I don't want to get rid of any of my things. They're mine. They're me."

Dr. Sparrow leans in. "That's just it, Maggie. The items you keep in your boxes and in your locker may feel important to you. But they are *not* you. They are just things."

"They feel like so much more."

"I know. No matter how much importance and feeling you attach to them, however, they're still just objects. Tossing them will feel hard at first. But, I promise, it'll get easier."

When I return home, I go to my room, and tear out a sheet of paper from my notebook. I take a pencil and draw a big rectangular chart with lots of rows and columns. One by one, I add all the stuff in my newest box. Then I make ten more charts for the objects in each one of the other boxes and one for the things in my locker. I rate each thing. The rating is hard. And there's a lot of erasing. But when I finish, I've made twelve charts and ranked every object. It feels like a big deal.

STUFF IN MY NEWEST BOX

STUFF	RATE	TOSSED	REWARD EARNED
3 milk cartons	5-worried to toss		10 points
5 Blue Bonnet gum wrappers	1-can toss, but not happy		2 points
3 bendy straws	2-can toss, but less happy		4 points
6 rocks	3-will toss, but hurts		6 points
3 sticks	4-don't want to toss		8 points
gecko necklace from Nana	10+-never tossing		infinity points
tassel from Nana's favorite scarf	8-can't let go		16 points
2 napkins	2-can toss, but less happy		4 points
yellow baby sock	9-hurts my heart to toss		18 points
2 butterscotch candy wrappers	5-worried to toss		10 points
diaper tabs	6-nervous to toss		12 points
piece from disposable bottle	6-nervous to toss		12 points
baby hair	9-hurts my heart to toss		18 points
button from Bud the Bear	9-hurts my heart to toss		18 points
yellow plastic fork and fireworks plate	3-will toss, but hurts		6 points
binkie with green frog	7-scared to toss		14 points
photos of Izzie	10+-never tossing		infinity points
threads from baby blanket	8-can't let go		16 points

Now comes the hardest part. The tossing. Dr. Sparrow said I should start with the things I rate the lowest. I pick up the foil gum wrappers. They were from the first Original Five squad practice. I remember that day. It was the start of the season in sixth grade. It had just stopped raining, and my hair was still damp. Dad gathered Ava, Gracie, Belle, Sam, and me together for a meeting in the red cabin and told us that we were going to be the first-ever all-girl trap squad from Fish, Fur, and Fly. We cheered, and then Ava passed out pieces of Blue Bonnet bubble gum. By the time we reached the shooting range, our lips and tongues were bright blue. I kept the gum wrappers. They feel important in my palm. Special. Meaningful. I wonder how I'm going to remember this without them.

When I was making the chart, I thought about the reward points. Mom and Dad suggested credit on MusicTunes, new sketch supplies, or the bike I saw at Landon's Bike Shop. It's way better than Dillon's hand-me-down. But I don't want any of those things.

I know what matters most. I'm saving for the

photo book I saw at Remember Me, the stationery store in the mall next to Candy King. It's leather with a gecko on the cover. Just like the one on the necklace from Nana. This is the reward that I want, to hold all the photographs of my baby sister. This is the book I want to keep forever. One of Dr. Sparrow's approved ways to save. This is where most of my tens will go.

But first, I have to toss my number ones.

I roll the wrappers between my thumb and pointer finger and walk out of my bedroom. The Dr. Sparrow plan is that all the stuff in the boxes gets tossed in the parent-approved garbage in the kitchen. With Mom or Dad watching. And no give-backs.

As I head down the stairs, my heart kicks up like it's turning on. Reminding me that it's paying attention. Promising me that it will remember.

When I step into the kitchen, it smells like chocolate. There's a we're-proud-of-you chocolate cake with chocolate icing and chocolate chips sitting in the middle of the table. It's from my parents. This is their thing. The other day when Charlie was going to stand up to Emma Rose at recess, they made a you've-got-this apple pie. Turns out, Charlie didn't actually stand up to Emma Rose that day, but the pie was amazing.

Mom and Dad are by the garbage, and Izzie is sleeping in her baby seat. Mom's wearing her practical gray sweater, and Dad's wearing his I-love-you smile. I look at my parents and my baby sister and want to turn around and run back into my room. I want to tuck the wrappers into the corner of my box, close the lid, and leave. I want to scream. But I can't. Because as much as I want to hold on tight and never let go, I don't ever want to feel the anger that clawed at my insides again.

I walk to the garbage in silence. The lid flips up like jaws opening wide. I count. There are five wrappers.

I will remember. I don't need these. And I don't need you, Cipher. Go away!

One wrapper falls from my fingers, and the silver foil floats on top of the leftover chicken parmesan. Then I let go of the second one. And the third. Until my hand is empty. I stare at the foil splayed across the tomato-basil sauce blanketing the garbage pile and close the lid.

I look down at the tiny human next to me. I kiss her forehead and whisper in her ear that I did it. I think she smiles. Then I sit down and take a slice of we're-proud-of-you chocolate cake.

31

Burn Baby Burn

During Beyond Poetry in English the next day, I wait for Mason to tell me why he wasn't at the last practice, but he doesn't.

Instead, he tells me that he found an alliteration. "What about 'Dunkin' Donuts'? That's like 'Peter Piper picked a peck of pickled peppers,' just shorter. Right?"

I nod and add it to our list. Which also now includes a metaphor from today's sports page, "Rigley Smith was a beast on the basketball court in last night's blowout game, scoring 48 points."

He's back on his laptop searching for more poetic stuff in the wild.

"So, you weren't at trap practice. Were you sick?" I ask.

"No," he says.

"Did you go away?"

"Nope."

"Have a hundredth birthday celebration for one of your great-grandparents?"

He shakes his head.

"Death of a great-aunt or your kid brother's play?"

His lip curls, snarl-like. "I wasn't sick. Don't have a kid brother. No one died or turned a hundred. Why are you asking me all this weird stuff?"

"I want to know what you did that was more important than coming to trap." I pause. "Or did you quit?"

"I'm not a quitter," he says.

"So why didn't you come?"

"Just couldn't make it." He turns back to search for more poetic things online.

"That's not good enough. We're a squad. That means something. We're not just some girls who shoot trap. We lost a squadmate to make room for you, so you need to show up."

He stares at me like there's something he wants to say.

I wait a long beat, but he says nothing. "Does this have to do with your dad?" I ask.

His steel-blue eyes tighten around me.

The bell rings for the end of class, and he walks away.

At lunch, I meet Ava and Sam at our usual lunch table. It's the one with the fewest gobs of old gum stuck to the bottom.

"Find Me is almost done." Ava takes a prototype sweater out of her backpack. "You put this on your dog. Then sign into the app. There's a coded strip sewn into the back of the sweater that shows your pet's location."

"It's so small," says Sam, adding hot sauce to her mac and cheese.

"This one's for Bruno. He's only about eleven pounds," Ava says.

"I definitely want one for Batman!" I say. "It just may need to be a bit bigger." I hand the sweater back to Ava.

"I'll make him a large blue one once we know the prototype works."

"Thanks," I say, swallowing a big gulp of my milk. "I stopped by Belle's the other day. You know, to see how she was about the whole trap thing."

"And?" Ava asks.

"She was fine. Which was good, but kind of surprising."

"I think it's weird that she doesn't care that she's not on the best team anymore," Sam says.

"She told me she likes that her new team is less intense and less competitive."

"Definitely weird." Sam sprinkles crunched-up potato chips into her now-spicy mac and cheese.

"Not any weirder than your mac and cheese," Ava says.

"I don't get why it doesn't bother her that we're not still together," I say. "You know, the Original Five."

"Maybe there's a chance she can still come back," Ava says, cutting her peanut-butter-and-fluff sandwich and giving me half. "What did you find out about Mason?"

"Nothing."

"You were partnered with him all of English, and he didn't say anything?" Sam asks before slurping her green Jell-O.

"He told me that he found an alliteration and a metaphor." I look at Sam and her jiggly dessert. "You know, dessert really shouldn't wiggle."

She smiles and slurps down the rest of the green slime.

"The entire time in class, he didn't say anything about why he wasn't at trap practice?" Ava asks.

I remember the look in his eyes today when I mentioned his father and the sort-of promise I'd made after his first practice not to tell my friends about how angry his dad got in the parking lot. "The only thing he said about trap was that he didn't quit."

Ava and Sam don't seem convinced, but they move on to arguing about what's better—peanut butter and fluff or mac and cheese with potato chips and hot sauce. I glance around the room to make sure no one's looking, tear off a small piece of the Burn Baby Burn hot sauce label, and slip it into my backpack.

32

Broken Promise

When I walk in the front door, Mom's waiting for me. She wants to know how my math test went and if we had mystery fish for lunch again. Then, as if it's as normal as asking me about my day, she tells me to empty my backpack. Another Dr. Sparrow thing—the bag check.

"The test was fine except for the last problem, which I didn't get to. And no mystery fish today." I start to walk away.

"Maggie," she says.

"What?"

"Your backpack. Please."

My body stiffens.

I hand my mom the bag and bite a hangnail on the pointer finger on my left hand. She pulls out my yellow geometry notebook, my dog-doodle-covered Spanish folder, my drawing of Izzie from art class . . . and the ripped red label from the Burn Baby Burn hot sauce.

She turns to me, looks at the label, then turns back to me. "Why don't you throw this away for bonus reward points?"

Sometimes I hate the chart. And the rules. And the tossing.

I take the torn label from my mom's hands and walk slowly over to the garbage can. Then stand there. Frozen. I tell Cipher to go away. To leave me alone. That I'll remember. That I don't need this stupid piece of paper.

I grit my teeth, open my palm, and toss my memories.

Just like that.

"I'm proud of you," I hear my mom say as I leave the kitchen.

The label reminded me of Mason. He was sitting in my sight at lunch. I wasn't spying. Not really. He was eating with Miguel and Robbie McGhee, who always introduces himself with his full name so now everyone just calls him Robbie McGhee. When Ava and Sam asked me about Mason, I caught him looking my way. I said nothing, finished my lunch, and then tucked the torn label into my backpack. Now it's in the trash. Gone. Forever.

I know this is the plan—Dr. Sparrow's plan, the one I agreed to. The one she promised would make the mad go away.

In my room, I lean over the plastic tub and watch my turtle happily swimming in his forever home. *He* won't make me throw anything away. I sit next to my newest box. Anchored. I slide in my earbuds and listen to "Closer to Fine" by the Indigo Girls, trying hard to believe their words. I peek into the box and survey my stuff.

Straws. Tassel. Necklace. Candy wrappers. Cartons. Hair. Threads. Tabs. Photos. Rocks. Sticks.

Wait!

I look again.

Bud the Bear's button is missing.

I check under me. Nothing.

Under the box. Nothing.

Under the bed. Nothing.

Worry flips in my gut. *Where is it?*

I check the other boxes under my bed.

Nothing.

The boxes in my closet.

Nothing.

Then I know what happened.

I leave my room. Pass Charlie building his Lego fort and Izzie sleeping in her bassinet. Stomp down the stairs. Mom's at the kitchen table on her computer.

"You broke your promise!" I yell, my mad spilling all over the kitchen.

"Honey, Dr. Sparrow said you'd need to share the contents of your bag at times. We discussed that." She closes her laptop.

"I'm not talking about the hot-sauce label."

"Then what?"

"You promised that you wouldn't go into my box! That you wouldn't touch my stuff!" My voice is loud and hollow.

She stares at me with the same wrinkled forehead

she had when Charlie told her that snakes don't have eyelids.

"You broke your promise! You went into my box! You took my Bud the Bear button!"

She shakes her head. "I wouldn't do that. I didn't break my promise. I didn't go into your box. I didn't take your things."

"We had a deal," I say, the tears falling off my cheeks onto the tile floor.

"And we still do," Mom says sternly with pursed lips and arms akimbo. "I didn't take anything, Maggie."

"I don't believe you!" I yell.

"Maybe you misplaced it or tucked it under something else. Either way, you need to calm down. And not speak to me from that angry place." She gets up from the table and takes a long, deep breath. "Let's look for it together."

"No!" I wipe my wet cheeks. "You can't fix this! You can't fix me!"

33

All of Me

I.

Need.

Space.

"I'm taking Batman for a walk," I tell my mom.

She exhales a big breath. "No, you're not. Not like this. Let's sit and talk."

"I don't want to talk."

"Then we can just sit quietly." I wonder if she learned this from Nana.

"I don't want to sit." A stretch of silence wedges between us. "With you."

"I get that. But right now, that's your only option.

You're not leaving this house upset." Mom's using her final-decision voice.

I close my eyes and count to twenty. Then I softly say, "Look, I'm not going to freak out." I know this is what Mom's worried about. Me totally losing it. Erupting. Again. I promise a million times that's not going to happen, but she still makes me sit for thirty minutes. The same amount of time I need to wait between eating and swimming. Then she talks to me about respect and the danger of accusing people of wrongdoing without all the facts.

I swallow my response, say I'm sorry I yelled, and play two rounds of Litmus on my phone at the kitchen table. When she sees I'm calm, she says, "You can go for a walk now, but I need you back home in thirty minutes to watch Charlie for me. I have to leave by four o'clock for an appointment. It's important. So bring your phone and don't lose track of time."

I nod.

The sun casts streaks across the trees as Batman and I walk down Vine Street. We weave around Greenwood, up Dudley, and down Kessler. I snap a picture on my phone of the sprawling oak at the corner of Puddingstone and Brookline. I think about its strong branches protecting Izzie, keeping her safe. I hope her forever family is like the oak.

We go past Piper's Pet Cemetery, around the high school football field, and to the park. I listen to Bob Dylan's "Blowin' in the Wind" on my headphones and wonder if he ever found the answers he was looking for. I take more pictures for Izzie—of the ducks, the dogs, the neighborhood. My neighborhood, which is also hers, even if it's only for a short bit. I check my watch. It's 3:45. Time to turn around. Retrace my route. Go home.

But I can't.

Not yet.

I keep going.

My cell rings. It's Mom. I ignore the call. I look around and realize I've wandered farther from home than I'd planned. Not on purpose. I guess. But I don't want to head back. Not yet. It's 3:55. I need more time.

I keep walking.

The sky splays a pink shadow across the sidewalk

as the sun moves across the sky. Batman and I pass a swing set, and I settle onto the middle swing as he rolls in the grass. The seat is low and green. It reminds me of the other day at the park with Mom, Dillon, Charlie, Izzie, and me. Dillon played basketball with some kids at the court. Mom and I took turns chasing Charlie through the tunnels and singing to Izzie. We all ended up by the swings. Dillon was daring me to go higher. Charlie was laughing as he pumped his legs faster and faster. Izzie was sleeping peacefully in Mom's arms. The memory tugs on my heart.

Mom calls again. It's 4:10. I don't answer. I turn off my phone and put it in my pocket.

34

Moon Days

Charlie always says that Batman is like the moon. They both have their own unique measure of time. One dog year equals one-seventh of a people year. One moon day equals twenty-nine Earth days. I wonder how much time in moon days I have left with Izzie.

As Batman and I leave the park, I look at my watch. It's 4:20. I was supposed to be home twenty minutes ago, and I'm still ten minutes away. The chill in the air crawls down my back. A sweet, floppy beagle across the street bays at Batman. The woman with the dog smiles at me. She reminds me of an older version of Mom with practical shoes.

"Good afternoon," Practical Shoes says.

I wave.

"Looks like you're the same age as my youngest grandkids. I have ten—no, eleven altogether. The last two are Joshua and Gregory." She opens her mailbox and riffles through the stack. "All bills. I used to love getting the mail, but no one writes letters anymore. A lost art." She closes her mailbox and pats her dog.

I start walking.

Turn on my phone.

Ten missed calls from Mom.

Ten worried messages.

When I step through the bright-blue front door at four thirty, Mom runs over, wraps me in her arms, and holds me tight. "Thank goodness you're okay." I feel the giant relief and stabbing fear from all the what-ifs that ran through her brain when I didn't answer the phone. "What happened? I tried calling, but it kept going right to voice mail."

Phone died. Lost track of time. Met a friend. Didn't mean to.

Guilt squeezes all my excuses.

I open my mouth and the truth shoots out. "I wasn't ready to forgive you. I needed more time."

Mom's angry eyebrows appear. The ones I saw after Batman ate the entire roast Mom had prepared for dinner when Dad's cousins visited from California.

"There's nothing to forgive. I didn't take your button. And I've never lied to you or broken a promise." Then, "What you did, Maggie, was irresponsible and dangerous. And it scared me. The truth is, it scared a lot of people. Me. Dad. Rita."

"You told Rita?"

Mom looks at her watch. "That was the appointment I had to go to. I was supposed to bring Izzie to Rita's."

"She's leaving today?" A heap of sadness replaces my anger.

Mom nods. "Just before you came downstairs, Rita called. I was going to tell you, but you were so upset about Bud and the button, I decided to wait until you came back from your walk. Which was supposed to be no more than thirty minutes."

Sorry.

"When you didn't come back, I had to call Rita and explain what was going on. I wasn't leaving this house until you came home. Dad was in a meeting and Dillon had practice. Maggie, I was worried. We were all worried."

"I'm sorry," I say, staring at my muddy sneakers and the carpet. I follow the lines on the carpet's pattern until they make me dizzy. I wonder if they lead to a place where I have a baby sister.

I peel the remaining mint-green polish off my nail. "Now what happens?" I ask.

"I need to bring Izzie to her new family as soon as I hear back from Rita. And you need to come with me. To apologize." Then she holds out her hand. "You've also lost phone privileges until you can show us that you're able to be more responsible."

I give my phone to my mother.

But I'm not ready to say good-bye.

I find Izzie, gently sweep her into my arms, and

sing "Lullaby Blue." Then I spread out Izzie's yellow blanket with the frogs and lay her down next to me. I think about Practical Shoes at her mailbox filled with bills, and I grab my purple pen and write. A letter.

Dear Izzie,

  I want you to know that I've loved being your big sister from the first moment I saw you in your mint green onesie and tiny yellow knit cap. Even if it was for just a little bit of time. You have the sweetest cry that doesn't even sound like a cry. Your eyes are this amazing blue color and your tiny head has this cute sprout of brown hair. And maybe my favorite thing about you is that your whole body smells like powder.

  I know you probably won't remember me, but I promise I'll never forget you.

  With love,
  Maggie
  Your big sister for a speck of time ☺

I fold my note and put it into a pink envelope. I seal it, write Izzie's name on the outside in all capital letters, and draw a big heart across the back.

Mom's talking on her cell. It's Rita. I hear Mom say that I'm back and okay. Then she hangs up the phone and tells me to get my coat. Dad's meeting ended. He's home and staying with Charlie. I'm going with her and Izzie to Caring Adoptions.

It's time.

To apologize.

In person.

On my way out the door, I grab my letter and the photos I printed for Izzie's Life Book. Then I pass a sleeping Batman in the checkered dog bed we got him from Box Mart.

Lying on the edge of Batman's bed is Bud the Bear's missing button.

35

Good-Bye, Little Bean

The car ride is quiet as we head to Rita's office. Mom's laser-focused on the road, Izzie's sleeping, and I'm listening to Marvin Gaye's "Mercy Mercy Me." Gramps introduced me to this song after Nana died. I listen until Mom pulls into a parking spot at the agency, turns off the engine, and leans toward me. I pull out my earbuds.

"I want you to remember that fostering babies is a gift," she says. "We get the privilege of taking care of these little ones and ensuring they get a good start in life."

I nod.

Mom takes my hands. "Izzie has made an imprint on our hearts. We won't forget her."

"I wish she wouldn't forget us," I say. *I wish she wouldn't forget me.*

"That's not why we foster, Maggie. We foster because these babies need love. And we have love to share."

"I brought the photos," I say, pulling out all the pictures I took for Izzie from her time with us.

"They're beautiful. And will be an important part of her story."

Then I say, "I'm sorry."

"I know," she says as she wipes the salty drops rolling down my cheeks.

I shake my head. "No, not about the walk."

Her look tells me that came out wrong.

"I mean, I *am* sorry about that, and the yelling, but I'm sorry about something else, too."

"What?" she asks.

"About Bud the Bear." Then a long pause filled with chunks of guilt. "I found the button on Batman's dog bed as we were leaving. *He* took it." I stare at my lap. "Not you."

She gives my hand an it's-going-to-be-okay squeeze. "Maggie, thinking something is true doesn't make it so. Even if you believe it with all your heart."

I bite my lip.

"You can't go around accusing people," she says. "It's incredibly hurtful."

The lump in my throat expands.

"I'm your mom. I've never lied to you, and I never will."

Then Rita's voice pours into our car. "Oh, thank goodness everyone's all right!"

Mom hugs me.

"I'm a fan of hugging," Rita says, "but we've got a baby to deliver."

Mom gives me the now-would-be-a-good-time-to-apologize look.

"Um, Rita. I'm, um, sorry that I messed up the plans."

Mom lifts a now-awake Izzie out of the car. Her eyes are wide-open. Like she knows something important is about to happen. As Mom snaps her car seat into the stroller, the wind blows her blanket off the top of the bag that's filled with her bottles, diapers, binkies, onesies, and a beanie. I run and get it.

"As long as our baby's fine, we're all gonna be fine," Rita says, winking at Mom. "Now, let's get this little one to her new family." She shoos the three of us inside.

We park Izzie's stroller at the door. Mom takes my little sister and asks me to stay in the waiting room for a bit while she and Rita introduce the adoptive couple to their new baby.

On the walls are photos of babies with notes attached. I read them all. Under a picture of a mom, a dad, a baby girl, and a yellow Lab, it says *Happy Holidays. Thanks for making our family complete. Love, Sage, Gabe, Rose, and Huey.* Once I get through the happily-ever-after wall of photos, I leaf through the pile of magazines on the table. *Parents. Adoptive Families. Working Mother.* On the bottom of the pile is the Caring Adoptions newsletter, and on the front page is a piece written by a girl named Amanda.

My name is Amanda, and I was adopted at birth. I'm writing to thank my birth mom for giving me the opportunities I've had in my life. We've never met, but as a seventeen-year-old, I recently realized she made an adoption plan for me *because* she loved me, not because she didn't. She loved me enough to know that I needed more than she could give. I know when the time is right, I will meet my birth mother, and when I do, I will begin by saying thank you.

Mom sticks her head out of the room and waves me in. It's time for the second half of my punishment. This half is way worse. Apologizing to the adoptive couple.

My legs feel stiff. I shuffle to the door and quietly walk into the conference room with the long wooden table. There's a vase with lilacs which fills the air with smells of love and possibility.

The two people across from me stand up. Asher is tall. At least six feet, with huge hands, lots of dark hair, and bushy eyebrows. Maya has long black hair tied in a ponytail, her eyes are like the night sky, and she smiles big as she holds Izzie close.

"Hi. I'm Maggie," I say as I sit in the seat next to Mom.

"My name's Asher, and this is Maya."

Mom nods to me.

I look at her and then the couple and say, "I'm sorry about today. I didn't mean to keep you waiting."

"Thank you," Asher says. "We're glad you're okay and just happy to have our little girl."

Their little girl.

"She's so incredibly beautiful." Asher smiles at Maya.

"And now we're a family," Maya says with happy eyes.

Izzie starts to cry. Maya pulls my baby sister close.

A piece of me is happy for Izzie. But there's another piece that wants to take her in my arms and sing to her.

Mom doesn't notice. She's busy sharing Izzie's

routine. When she eats, sleeps, and bathes. How much she eats, sleeps, and bathes.

Asher writes down every word Mom says about Izzie's care.

"And if she's crying," I say, "she likes to be held high on your shoulder while you sing 'Lullaby Blue.'"

Asher and Maya look at each other and then at me. "We don't know that song," Maya says.

Right there in the middle of the conference room with the long wooden table and the yellow flowers, I sing "Lullaby Blue." Asher scribbles down the words while Maya hums in Izzie's ear. They seem excited and nervous, and I forget that I'm sad.

"These are for Izzie." I slide the photos across the table.

Asher picks them up. "They're beautiful. We'll put them in her Life Book so she knows her whole story from the day she was brought into this world."

"And this." I put the pink envelope on the table.

"We'll be sure she gets this, too," Maya says in a voice coated with softness. Then, "I know you call her Izzie. That's lovely."

I smile.

"We plan to name her after Asher's mother who passed away two years ago."

I look over at Izzie. She makes sweet little sucking noises.

"Her name will be Delilah," Maya says.

"That's beautiful," my mom says.

I squeeze the frog binkie that I put in my pocket on the way out of the house. The one Mom doesn't know I brought.

"But I do think Isabelle would be a beautiful middle name," Asher says.

Happiness hugs me, and I ask if I can hold her one more time to say good-bye.

Maya hands me this perfect tiny human. I hold her close and whisper in her ear. "You're going to a new home and a new family. But know that in my heart, you'll always be my little sister. I love you. Good-bye, Little Bean."

Then I hand my baby sister to her forever family and walk out the door.

36

One More Little Human

The drive back from the agency is filled with holes and missing. When we get home, Charlie hugs me tight.

"Want to build a Lego castle?" he asks.

I shake my head.

"Want to play Litmus?" Dad asks.

"No, thanks. I really want to go to Wade's Pond. Is that okay?"

"How about we all go?" Mom says.

I bite my lip. "I kind of want some time alone." My parents look at each other. "I know I made a mistake earlier today. A really big one. But that won't happen again. I cross-my-heart promise to be back in an hour."

They exchange another glance.

"Please," I say.

"You have exactly one hour," Mom tells me.

I grab my bike and pedal fast to the pond. When I get there, I set the alarm on my watch for forty-five minutes. I don't want to chance being even one minute late. I take out my Go On, Change the World! notebook from my backpack, sit on a tree stump, slip in my earbuds, and close my eyes.

The wind kisses my cheeks, and all I see is Izzie. The baby who used to be my sister. The baby who smelled like powder. The baby who is not my baby anymore. The sadness squeezes my heart like the ivy that grows tight around the maple tree at the edge of the pond. I open my eyes and draw everything I can remember about Izzie's tiny nose, round face, and sprout of brown hair. The tears flow, but I don't stop. I need to remember. I don't want to let go.

As I draw, I wonder if this empty feeling will ever go away. And if it does, will the memories go with it?

My alarm buzzes. My time's up.

I hop on my bike and get home before the one-hour mark. Mom and Dad are in the family room playing Litmus with Charlie and Dillon. The category is music. I'm still not ready to join in.

I can't pretend everything is normal.

I can't pretend our family of five didn't have one more little human this morning.

The next day, Ava stops over after school. We're hanging with Bert when she reaches into her jacket and hands me a small cardboard box with a blue ribbon.

"What's this for?" I ask.

"Just open it," she says.

I take off the bow and lift the lid. Sitting in the middle of the box is a necklace with a silver heart charm. On it is an inscription: TO MAGGIE, MY BFF WITH THE BIGGEST HEART.

I hug Ava, slip on my necklace, and look in the mirror. "Thank you. It's beautiful."

"What's beautiful?" Charlie wants to know.

I walk over and show him my gift. His brown eyes grow big. "It's pretty. And shiny."

"Thanks, Bear."

"But it's not your birthday," he says.

"I know. It's a just-because present." I run my fingers along the charm, remembering the gecko necklace from Nana.

"I knew your sister was feeling sad," Ava says.

"Because Izzie isn't our sister for keeps anymore?" Charlie asks.

"Yep. I thought this would make her feel better."

"Does it?" Charlie says. "Can jewelry do that?"

I nod.

Ava looks at me. "Jewelry might not have magical powers. But your sister does have a great big heart."

A warmth runs through me like a cup of hot cider with cinnamon.

"Do you know who has the biggest heart in the entire world?" Charlie asks.

"You?" I answer.

Charlie shakes his head.

"Batman?" Ava says.

Charlie laughs.

"Bert?"

"Nope. A blue whale," he says, then darts off down the stairs.

Ava turns to me. "Okay, so maybe you have the second-biggest heart."

37

Remember Me

Dr. Sparrow's office smells like buffalo chicken. I can't believe it's been four days since I said a forever good-bye to Izzie. My heart still hurts in the place where she used to be. It's like a dark well. Today, the girl with the long, shiny braid is in the waiting room when I get there. This time, she doesn't look sad. The man I think is her dad is talking on his cell under a sign that says THANK YOU FOR TURNING OFF YOUR PHONES. I move into the seat next to my waiting-room friend.

I offer her a stick of gum and wait to see if she keeps the wrapper, but she doesn't. She tosses it into the trash and then tells me about her dog named Lou, an Australian shepherd puppy who keeps eating her sneakers. She shows me the back of one of her green high-tops, which has a chunk missing from the heel.

I want to show her a picture of Batman and Bert, but I realize I don't have phone privileges back yet. Before I can tell her about the time Batman ate through the insulation of our house, it's my turn.

Dr. Sparrow rolls her spinning chair from behind her big wooden desk so she's sitting across from me. Just me. Mom's in the waiting room, reading a student's college essay about cooking menemen with her Turkish grandmother. Dr. Sparrow's neck is decorated with a bright-pink polka-dot scarf.

"How are you today?" she asks.

"Izzie isn't Izzie anymore," I say, trying not to blink. Because if I do, I know the tears will flow, and I'm not sure I'll be able to stop them. "She's Delilah."

"That must be hard."

"It is." I interlock my fingers and squeeze tight. "I promised Izzie that I'd remember her, but I'm so scared I'll forget." I let out a big breath I didn't know I was holding.

"Have you?"

"No, but what if I do?"

"Your brain will help you remember the things in life that are important to you. I promise," Dr. Sparrow says.

"But Nana's brain didn't help her remember the things in life that were important," I say. Then, in the smallest of voices, "Like me." My mouth twists in the way it does when I'm thinking and feeling a lot at the same time.

"Maggie, I know that was hard. Really hard. But you're a healthy twelve-year-old who can make, keep, and recall memories."

I nod.

"I need you to trust the process . . . and me," Dr. Sparrow says.

"I do. Most of the time. I just miss Izzie and wish she'd remember me."

"The photos you took and the letter you wrote will be a part of her Life Book. But the truth is, Maggie, sometimes we do a wonderful thing just because we can. Because it's the right thing to do. Not because we'll be remembered for it."

I know she's right, but that doesn't make the sad feeling of missing disappear.

When I get home, I walk to Gramps's house.

He's sitting in Nana's folding chair in the backyard. I show him my photo album. "What do you do when you miss Nana?" I ask.

"This, I guess," he says. "I like to have her around me. So I sit in her green chair, read her celebrity magazines, and garden." He laughs. "And sometimes I spray her perfume in the air just to keep me company."

"I was going to say that you smell good."

His smile shines. "Thanks."

"I know Izzie was only with us for a speck of time, but I miss her huge."

"Love has a way of taking hold." He walks over to the tilting tomato plants and hands me a stake. I push it into the ground, cut a sliver of white twine, and tie up the tops of the drooping plants. "Now, to keep the rabbits away."

This is the same battle Nana used to fight. She'd say, "Don't let their cuteness fool you. Those bunnies will eat your entire garden." Gramps and I each take an end of the chicken-wire fence he bought at Box Mart, unravel it around the garden, and then secure it in place.

Gramps steps back. "That should do it."

"Nana would be proud. The garden looks good," I say. "You haven't killed anything."

He laughs.

When I get home, I smell like a basil-and-tomato salad. Batman prefers an all-bacon scent but licks my face anyway.

Today's entry in my Go On, Change the World! notebook:

1. Eat fresh tomatoes.
2. Don't trust cute bunnies.
3. Be brave, like Gramps.

38

Skip It

After school the following week, I hop on my bike and ride to the pond. I try not to think about the two napkins I have to toss today or the hole in my heart where Izzie used to be. I ride down Queens Drive, across Baron, and cut through the path by Sycamore Lane. I crouch down low to miss the overgrown vines with the prickers. Last time I took the shortcut, I forgot to crouch, and ended up with scratches all over my shoulders. I looked like I'd been attacked by the big fat cat with emerald eyes that slinks around the neighborhood. Dillon calls him Voldemort.

The cool air feels good on my cheeks. I slow down as I get closer to the pond. I lean my bike on the maple dressed in red leaves and pick up the perfect stone with a flat side. Dad showed me and Dillon and Charlie how to skip rocks at the beach last summer. Dillon got his to skip four times, mine skipped twice, and Charlie's sank. I flip the stone and it splashes once. Then another stone skids past mine. I turn around.

It's Mason.

"What are you doing here?" I ask. I've always thought of this place as my spot. The thick canopy of leaves and branches keeps it hidden.

Mason shrugs. "My dad's at work. I didn't feel like going back to an empty house. And we don't have trap practice today." Then he looks at me. "What about you?"

"Just like it here." I first came to the pond by accident. I was riding my bike and trying to keep up with Dillon when I took a wrong turn. And landed at this place. It was quiet and beautiful. And felt like it was all mine. Until now.

"Yeah, me too." He smiles.

I guess I could share.

"Those are really good," I say, pointing to his sketch pad.

He says thanks, and we move on to talking about skipping stones and trap. And the burger with a fried egg and lots of hot sauce at The Burger Shack. Apparently, both of our favorite.

"I found another one of those things for the Beyond Poetry assignment. There's a sign in the window at Mac's Pizza that says BEST PIZZA EVER. Total hyperbole. I mean, it's good, but best ever? That's questionable," I say.

"I've never had a slice there," Mason says. "Just their steak-and-cheese sub with onions and peppers. And that *could* qualify as best ever."

I grab a stone and then swap it for one with a flatter side. "Do you think your dad will come around to your being on our squad?" I ask.

He looks at me. "Doubt it." He glides a smooth gray stone across the water. Five hops.

We skip stones for a while longer. Mostly without words. My thoughts flood with Izzie. I think about her slender fingers and the smell of powder. I wonder what she's doing now. And if Maya and Asher remember the words to "Lullaby Blue."

"I actually need to head back home. Promised my little brother I'd take him to the park." I look around and realize Mason walked here. "Where do you live?" I ask.

"On Dudley," he says, tossing a handful of acorns into the pond, creating a chain of ripples.

"Want a ride? That's not far from my house."

"*You're* going to give *me* a ride?" he says with a half laugh.

"Unless you'd rather walk."

He takes a second to climb onto the back of my orange-and-black hand-me-down bike and holds on to my waist. It's kind of awkward but kind of okay.

"Before I drop you off, I need to stop at my house to check in with my mom." In person. I don't say this is part of my punishment for worrying my parents.

"Sure. It's not like anyone's waiting on me at home."

When we walk through the bright-blue door, Mom's working at the kitchen table and Charlie's standing there with a fistful of worms.

"Hey, Bear, why the worms?"

"They're for Bert. He's hungry," Charlie says. Then, "Are you ready to go?" He shows me the time on his watch.

"Soon. I just need to take my friend home first. This is Mason."

"Hi. I'm Charlie and these are for Maggie's turtle," he says, sticking the worms in Mason's face. "Bert is a forever pet," he says. "My little sister wasn't a forever sister."

I wrap my brother in a love-you hug.

"Didn't know you had a little sister," Mason says.

"We don't," Charlie says. "We borrowed her and then had to give her back."

I can't believe it's been two weeks since she went to her forever family.

"Her name was Izzie," I say. "She was our foster sister."

Think that's the first time I've ever said those words out loud.

Our. Foster. Sister.

My. Foster. Sister.

39

A Really Good Thing

Dad adds another practice to the trap schedule. We have a little over two weeks until the state tournament, and he wants us to feel ready. "And confident," he says.

In the truck, I put in my earbuds and listen to Julia Brennan's "Inner Demons." I'm certain that Cipher's my demon. Just not sure who my angels are.

Before I can figure it out, Dad pulls into the parking lot of The Baking Room. From behind the counter, Ida lets me try the chocolate-peanut-butter brownies as if I don't already know they're melt-in-your-mouth delicious. When I smile and nod, she fills Dad's bakery box with a dozen.

In the car, I twist the twine from the box in my fingers, willing myself to remember this moment without the string. Then I let go of the twine, put the brownies in the back seat, pop in my earbuds, and stare out the window.

At practice, Dad starts a fire in the wood-burning stove in the red cabin to erase the chill in the air. Ava, Sam, and Gracie put on their vests and grab their eye protection and earplugs. I unzip my bag, take out my trap stuff, and quietly tuck a small green ribbon into my pocket. It's Belle's. I spied it on the floor that day I went over to her house to make sure she was okay. It must have fallen out of her hair during the dance party. I slid it into my backpack and, when I got home, put it with my trap stuff. I thought she should be here with us, and this way, she kind of is.

Mason's alone over by the fake green plants on the right side of the room. His messy dark hair is gelled back today. I walk over with the box from The Baking Room. Nothing says *team* like warm brownies. Everyone moves toward the smell of peanut butter and chocolate.

Dad starts practice with an announcement. "The morning of the state tournament, we'll be leaving at seven o'clock and traveling as a squad in one of the club's vans."

I see Mason look away and wonder if his father will let him go.

My dad finishes with his safety tip reminders and our squad heads to field one. The clay discs are already loaded. I take position one, and Mason, Ava, Gracie, and Sam find their spots.

"Eyes and ears!" I call, then look around to make sure everyone has their eye protection on and their earplugs in. Ava has new safety glasses, they're green, like her earplugs and socks.

I mount my gun, press my cheek into its cold, hard side, and dig the butt squarely into my shoulder. It feels easier and lighter since I've been doing the push-ups and pull-ups.

"Pull!" I yell, waiting for the neon orange to find me. After a few seconds, there it is. Bright and beautiful!

I see it.

I feel it.

I hit it.

It shatters like fireworks in the sky. I feel the rhythm and precision of the moment. My insides warm and dance.

Ava gets a 25/25. Which is a huge deal! She'll finally get her 25 patch, and our vests will match. I hug her tight. But Sam ends up with only 13. She's not happy. At all. Dad talks to her about switching her stance, trying something different. All she says is how much she hates steel shells.

I agree the lead ones make it a lot easier to shatter the clay discs. I used them once. But we can't use them at our range because it's protected. It's over a pond, and if the lead gets into the water, it could poison the wildlife. Like Bert.

"I'm worried about Sam," I say to Ava.

"Me too. It's got to be hard. Especially since her little sister just keeps getting better. At everything."

I nod, and as I walk over to Sam, I ask the universe to please take care of her. Then I offer her a second brownie. I know it won't make her shoot better, but maybe it'll make her feel better.

"You've got this," I say to Sam.

"Not likely," she says, walking away.

Later that afternoon, Mom, Dad, and I head to Dr. Sparrow's office. I go in first. Alone. I tell Dr. Sparrow the things I've tossed and how much I hate the trash can.

"I know this is difficult," she says. "But you're moving in a positive direction."

"I guess. Like my whole body isn't as sad as it was eighteen days ago, when I said my forever good-bye."

"Exactly. That's progress," Dr. Sparrow says.

"But, true confession, there are still times I worry that I'll forget. Everything." I look down at my hands.

"That's okay. As we've discussed, this is a process. And it takes time."

I nod, wanting so badly to believe that someone wearing a bright-yellow sweater with tulips wouldn't lie.

Then I take out the phone my parents returned to

me last night and show Dr. Sparrow my new playlist. She's a jazz fan. But says any music is a good distraction when Cipher shows up. We listen to "Mr. Tambourine Man" while we wait for Mom and Dad to join us. They told me last night they wanted a few minutes to talk with me and Dr. Sparrow today.

They both smile when they walk in and hear Dad's favorite song playing.

"We are so proud of Maggie," Mom says.

Dr. Sparrow enthusiastically agrees.

Then Mom clears her throat. "But we're also worried." She looks over at me. "Maggie has already started talking about fostering again, and we feel it may just be too hard."

For me.

"I absolutely disagree," I say. "I think another baby would be a good thing. A really good thing."

For me.

I fold my arms across my chest.

Dr. Sparrow listens intently. "I understand your desire to foster again, Maggie, and your parents' concerns. For now, you need to focus on overcoming the worries that cause you to collect and keep things. You need to learn to let go. Of people and things. Without the fear that you'll also be letting go of the memories you cherish."

When the appointment ends, I tell my parents that I still think they're wrong about fostering again.

"I know," Dad says. "And that's okay."

"Let's put all our energy into Dr. Sparrow's plan," Mom says as she pulls the car into the mall parking lot. "We saw your charts this morning. You've earned your first reward."

My frustration slips behind a sliver of pride.

In Remember Me, there are gift cards and stationery and YOU ARE THE BEST mugs, and pillows and pencil cases and puzzles, and notepads in rainbow colors. Then I see what I want. It's on the table in front of me, the journal with the gecko on the cover. I look at my parents and smile. This is it. And it's beautiful.

That night, I fill the book with all the photos I took of Izzie.

When she was still my baby sister.

40

Rock Day

The ants are gone, and my boxes are getting lighter. Every day. Even my locker is less stuffed. I let go of the napkins and milk cartons. Each time I toss something else, I tell myself its story. The name-that-dish mystery meal with Ava and Sam that we ate blindfolded, the milk from the first day with Izzie, and the napkin from the last. I think about Taco Tuesday or Fish Friday or Meatball Monday. Who I sat with. What we talked about. I replay each of these moments so I won't forget.

Today is Rock Day.

I need to throw away the smooth rocks from the pond and the ones from my walks with Charlie. I don't want to. I want to keep them with me. But I don't ever want to feel the ugly anger that tore at my insides. I roll the stones between my palms. I know Mom or Dad will be at the garbage can, watching, so I can't just pretend to toss.

I donate a few to Bert's tub. I decide that's not cheating. It's helping Bert have a happier home. I set down the speckled stone from the walk in the woods with Charlie and Izzie, the smooth skipping stone from the pond, and the almost-white one from the beach at low tide, when Batman ate three dead crabs, then puked. I walk down to the garbage. Mom's waiting for me by the trash can with her hair tucked behind her ears.

"Ready?" she says.

I nod and, in my head, talk back to Cipher.

Leave me alone! I don't need you. I don't need these rocks. I will remember anyway.

I walk over to the metal trash can, open its jaws, and throw my rocks on top of the asparagus Charlie refused to eat last night. A combination of way-to-go and don't-forget fills me.

Mixed feelings are confusing. They tug at all different parts of me. At the same time.

When I'm done tossing, I cross it off the chart for my newest box.

I spread the other eleven charts on the floor in front of me and look at all the x's. Each day, I toss something from a different box. Yesterday, it was my old purple toothbrush that played the "Happy Birthday" song. The day before, it was the empty cup from the lemon slush, which I'd been saving in a box in the back of my closet. I got the slush the day I went to Maker Farms with Gramps. It was the best afternoon. A mama cow and her baby had just moved to the farm, and the owners were holding a naming contest for the calf.

I filled out an entry slip and found out a week later that Ruby was chosen to be the name of the youngest resident of Maker Farms.

STUFF	RATE	TOSSED	REWARD EARNED
3 milk cartons	5-worried to toss	X	10 points
5 Blue Bonnet gum wrappers	1-can toss, but not happy	X	2 points
3 bendy straws	2-can toss, but less happy	X	4 points
6 rocks	3-will toss, but hurts	X	6 points
3 sticks	4-don't want to toss		8 points
gecko necklace from Nana	10+-never tossing		infinity points
tassel from Nana's favorite scarf	8-can't let go		16 points
2 napkins	2-can toss, but less happy	X	4 points
yellow baby sock	9-hurts my heart to toss		18 points
2 butterscotch candy wrappers	5-worried to toss		10 points
diaper tabs	6-nervous to toss		12 points
piece from disposable bottle	6-nervous to toss		12 points
baby hair	9-hurts my heart to toss		18 points
button from Bud the Bear	9-hurts my heart to toss		18 points
yellow plastic fork and fireworks plate	3-will toss, but hurts	X	6 points
binkie with green frog	7-scared to toss		14 points
photos of Izzie	10+-never tossing		infinity points
threads from baby blanket	8-can't let go		16 points

41

Worth Missing

The next day, Dad, Mom, Dillon, Charlie, and I are huddled on the couch under Nana's blue afghan, playing Litmus on Dad's tablet. The category is presidents. Dad's the house champion of all things presidential. The electronic board displays the question: Where in the Constitution are the qualifications for the president set out?

Dad: "Article Two, Section One, Paragraph Five."

Next: Which president had the nickname "The Last Cocked Hat"? Stroking his beard, Dad says, "James Monroe." But it's Charlie's turn and he guesses Andrew Johnson.

"Andrew Johnson is wrong," the computer voice declares. "The correct answer was James Monroe."

We play until dinner, then dive into happy, mad, sad. It's Soup Sunday, which turns out to be all of our happy. My sad is the empty hole left by Izzie, and my mad is Cipher. I don't share that last one.

After dinner, I tell my parents again that I think we should foster another baby. They look at each other and say, "We'll see." Which usually means no. Like when Charlie wanted an ant farm.

I visit my boxes and replay my Izzie memories in my head. I'm starting to believe that Dr. Sparrow is right. That I'll remember the things that are important to me. That they won't get lost like keys and phones and Mom's reading glasses.

The next morning, I stop in what was Izzie's room. When I close my eyes, I can see her lying in the bassinet in her yellow onesie.

At school, Mason's not in English or at his usual lunch table.

When the bell sounds at the end of the day, I hop on my bike and follow the path down the gravel and dirt, through the prickers, to Wade's Pond. The frogs sound like really bad band practice.

When I get there, Mason's sitting on the stump closest to the pond skipping rocks. "Where were you today?" I ask.

"Sick," he says.

"You don't look sick," I say, sitting next to him. That's when I see pages and pages of cartoonlike drawings of birds and squirrels. And one of a girl. With wild hair.

He stuffs the sketches into his backpack and grabs a flat, muddied rock from under the brush.

We skip stones in quiet for a while, surrounded by a cool breeze and the smell of pines. "I like to draw, too," I say. "Not like you. Mostly just faces. Like in Mr. Rodriguez's art class. The other day, I drew one of Izzie, the baby we were fostering. Mr. Rodriguez said she looked like me."

Then Mason's eyes catch mine. "Was it hard when she left?" he asks.

"Not for Dillon," I say.

"What about for you?"

I take a gulp of pond air, nod yes, and look away to hide the tears I know are rolling down my cheeks. "I miss her." My rock skips two times.

"Think you guys will get another foster kid?"

"Don't know. I want to, but my parents don't think it's a good idea. They think it might be too hard. But I think they're wrong. I mean, some people are just worth missing. Like my nana. And Izzie."

Mason nods. "And my mom."

"Where's she?" I ask, handing him a rock with a smooth, flat edge.

"She died about a year after my parents got divorced."

His voice cracks and his eyes brim with sadness.

"Things were rough between them. She'd met someone else and moved out. That's why my dad hates trap."

"I thought he just hated it because we were an all-girl team who he thought stunk?" I see a small stone on the ground and stuff it in my pocket. For later.

"That's part of it. But for him, it's not about the

all-girl thing or winning." He pauses. "It's about my mom. She shot trap."

"Oh."

"And now, it reminds him of her. That's why he wants me to stop." His voice cracks again.

He grabs a flat gray rock and sails it across the pond. Six skips.

"And that's why I can't."

In that moment, I realize I'm not the only one who doesn't want to forget.

42

The Fabric of Things

At the end of trap, Dad congratulates Ava on her 25/25 at practice the other day.

"Today we celebrate," he says. Then Ava tosses her cap in the air, and the whole team shoots holes in it. This is one of my favorite trap traditions. Dad still has his 25/25 hat. And I have mine. It hangs in my room right next to the sketch I drew of Izzie.

Dad thanks everyone for a good practice and packs up the gear.

I put my trap stuff in my bag and walk over to Ava. "Congrats again."

"Thanks," she says, holding her holey hat. "Do

you want to come over? I think I've figured out the coding for the Find Me sweater."

"I can't come now. I'm meeting my brothers at my grandfather's house for his famous Grandkids' Pizza Night. The one with fresh basil and tomatoes from the garden."

That's mostly true, except for leaving out that I also have an appointment with Dr. Sparrow.

Ava nods. She's had Gramps's pizza before.

"But I'll come later and bring Batman," I say. "We can try it out on him."

Dad drives me to Dr. Sparrow's office. When we get there, I'm surprised that I'm not dreading seeing her. That I'm kind of looking forward to guessing what bright-colored sweater or scarf she's wearing. Today, it's magenta. I ask her if she does this on purpose. "You know," I say, "like the kids who come in here can't hate talking to some-one who's always wearing happy-color clothes."

She just laughs.

We talk for a while about the things I've tossed.

How it's getting easier to let go.

And not forget.

When I get home, I ride my bike to Gramps's for Pizza Night. When I get to the end of his driveway, I find my grandfather and brothers in the backyard. Gramps already has a basket of tomatoes for the pizza. Then I spy a shoebox in Charlie's hands.

"Why do you have the box from your new sneakers?" I ask, walking over to my little brother.

"Bert wanted to come with us," Charlie says as if no more explanation is needed.

I look at Dillon. "We couldn't find the thing you carry him in. So we made our own," he says.

"But don't worry, we gave him lots of worms and lettuce and water." Charlie opens the lid to show me Bert's temporary home.

Gramps interrupts. "Charlie, can you grab me a new roll of twine from the kitchen?"

"But I was just going to show Dillon how tall I am compared to the tomato plants," he says.

"You can—"

"It's okay. I'll do it," I say to my brothers. "Just keep your eye on Bert."

When I walk into the kitchen, it smells like

Gramps's special pizza sauce. I see the glass jar of dried flowers on the counter right between the three-tier-castle clock and the lemon dish detergent, like it's just part of the fabric of things. The mixer clock chimes as I search the drawer and cabinets and pantry. I find lots of pens and paper clips and jalapeño chips. But no twine.

"Gramps," I yell out the screen door. "I don't see any more of that string. Are you sure it's in here?"

"I thought I got some at Maker Farms when I bought more plant food. But hold on a sec. I'm coming in to check," he says as he walks into the kitchen. After a hunt that includes his bedroom, the pantry, and under the bathroom sink, he finally finds a roll in the garage in a bin marked EXTENSION CORDS.

"We're the victors of the twine," I say, carrying the new roll. But the backyard is empty. Then I hear the basketball bouncing and see Dillon and Charlie dribbling down the driveway.

I run over with the twine, steal the ball from Dillon, and pass to Charlie for a layup. I high-five my little brother, who then does cartwheels up and down the driveway.

I flop down on the grass, laughing with my brothers. I look around. "Where's Bert?"

Charlie and Dillon point to the shoebox on the grass.

It's toppled over. And the lid is off.

The words I want to say tangle with fear.

I run over to the shoebox.

It's empty.

Bert is gone.

43

Unicorns

I run from one end of the yard to the other. Back and forth and back and forth.

"Bert," I yell in a voice filled with worry.

I crawl on my hands and knees under the bushes. Around the rock garden. Through the patch of dandelions. Nothing.

"I'm a good finder, Maggie. Don't worry," Charlie says in his sweet little-brother voice. The one that still believes in unicorns.

But I *am* worried. I've circled the lawn three times. No Bert.

Then I stop and look at Dillon. "This is your fault!"

He doesn't respond.

"I told you guys to watch him. I told you he's fast. And now, he could be anywhere," I yell, my arms stretched out to the corners of the yard.

Dillon looks at me, but there's nothing to say. Bert is gone.

Dillon does another search under the bushes, in the weeds, and along the bed of wildflowers. Gramps walks the perimeter of the yard.

I stand and survey the grass. *Where could he be?* I don't see his shell, or moving blades of grass or rustling leaves. Goose bumps climb onto my skin.

Fear taps my insides.

I run back into the house and grab the emergency in-case-the-lights-go-out flashlight and some squash. Bert loves squash. I run the squash along the grass, hoping maybe he'll smell it and come back to me.

I wait. And wait.

But he doesn't.

"Hey there." I turn around. It's Dad. "Gramps told me what happened." He folds me into his arms, and I let the worry melt into his Go On, Change the

World! sweatshirt. He holds me tight until my cries slow-roll to a stop.

"It's getting late. We need to go home now," Dad says. "I put your bike in my car, and we can look again tomorrow."

I step back. "I can't leave Bert. Not now." The desperation clings to my words.

"Honey, you have to."

"I don't. He's not like one of those things on my chart. You can't make me let *him* go." My body starts to shiver and shake.

Dillon comes over. "We'll head home and make a plan. I promise, I'll come back here with you tomorrow," he says.

"I'm sorry," Charlie says, hugging my waist.

"Me too," Dillon says.

The car ride home is pin-drop quiet. No music. No talking. No random facts.

When we get to the house, Dad puts the pizza we never ate on the kitchen table. I don't want any. My hunger left with Bert.

I run to my room and hug my boxes. Then I grab

my Go On, Change the World! notebook, my purple pen, and write:

> 1. Turtles can run away.
> 2. Brothers can't be trusted.
> 3. Everything leaves.

I stare at the moon, listen to "You Can't Count
On Me" by Counting Crows, and tell Bert, wher-
ever he is, that I'm sorry. My mind trails back to the
day I brought him home. It was warm and sunny. I
look out my window. I see the North Star and make
a wish. Put it in the universe. For Bert and Izzie.

There's a knock on my door. It's Dillon and Charlie.

With another apology. A plan. And a card. Decorated with blue glitter and a moon.

I go back to my Go On, Change the World! list.

> 1. Turtles can run away.
> 2. ~~Brothers can't be trusted.~~ Forgive brothers.
> 3. ~~Everything leaves.~~ Find Bert.

I go to sleep wondering if Bert and Izzie are looking at the moon.

44

Shell and All

I wake to the warm sun streaming in through the gaps in my shutters. It takes me a stretch and a few eye blinks to remember that Bert is gone. I pop out of bed, toss on sweatpants, and hug Batman.

I skip breakfast and run smack into Charlie as I'm about to get my bike.

"Where are you going?" he asks.

"To find Bert."

"I'm coming with you," he says. "You need your best finder. And that's me." He slips his little hand in mine. "Plus, I'm wearing my lucky shirt." It's white with a picture of a four-leaf clover on the front.

I'm about to squeeze all his sweetness when I hear a loud honk. "Get in," Mom says as she opens the door to her silver SUV. "Dad and Dillon are already at Gramps's house."

I remember Dillon's plan. But thought it wouldn't happen when I realized it's Saturday. I'd already told Dad that I was skipping practice, but never thought Dillon would miss basketball. Even after he got three teeth pulled, he ran up and down the court with tissues stuffed in the bloody gaps where his teeth had been.

When I get to Gramps's house, there are doughnuts on a big round platter on the wooden table, and the red tea kettle is whistling. Gramps hugs me close and serves himself some mint tea with honey. On the table are stacks of flyers with Bert's photo and the word *missing*. I thank him for creating these, and he tells me that Dillon was the one who made them. Salty tears drizzle onto my chocolate glazed doughnut.

"I've mapped out the neighborhood," Dillon says, spreading a poster replica of the neighborhood on

Gramps's kitchen table. "We'll divide up the streets and hand out flyers to every family."

"Don't you have practice?" I ask.

"I told my coach I couldn't make it," Dillon says.

In this moment, I'm glad I have a big brother.

Even if he lost my turtle.

"What about trap?" I ask Dad.

"Coach Aiden is running practice today." He puts his hands on my shoulders and says, "We're all exactly where we need to be."

Dillon takes a handful of flyers and heads to Landview Lane and the nearby pond. Dad and Mom want to come with me, but I tell them what I really want is for us to canvass as much of the neighborhood as possible in the shortest amount of time. And that means splitting up.

Mom and Dad look at each other and do that thing where they have a conversation without speaking. I wonder if that's something all parents do.

Then Mom says, "Okay. But keep your phone on and stay on Brookville Drive."

I promise. Mom takes Charlie to Bannister Way,

Dad goes toward Lancaster Lane, Gramps wanders the yard in case Bert returns, and Batman and I head to the homes along Brookville, near the farmers' market. The smell of freshly roasted peanuts and caramel-covered apples compete for air space. But it does nothing for the big fat missing that's settled into my heart.

I walk up the path to the brick house on the right. *Knock knock*. Nothing. *Knock knock* again. Nothing. I take my flyer and slide it into their mailbox and put up the red flag.

Next stop: a ranch house with crooked black shutters and overgrown bushes. If I weren't so sad, I'd be scared. This is the one house that Dillon and I avoid when we go trick-or-treating. It looks dark and abandoned. Like no one loved it enough. But today, I need this house.

Knock knock.

It's quiet.

Knock knock.

I wait.

Knock—

I hear footsteps and hold my breath. The door

opens. Just a crack. Jagged fingers hang on the doorframe.

"What do you want?" says a small, raspy voice.

"I, um, wondered if, um, you've seen a turtle. His name's Bert." I hold out the flyer.

The jagged hand pushes open the door farther. Standing there is a woman with a tiny face of layered wrinkles.

Batman licks her hand.

"What's his name?" she asks.

"Batman."

She digs her hand into her front pocket, pulls out a dog treat, and hands it to Batman. "Well, I haven't seen any turtles," she says. "They're not usually roaming the neighborhood. I mean, there are cars around. Them things could get run over. Shell and all."

I swallow the hurt that flows from her words and walk to the next house. There are yellow and red and green balloons tied to the doorknob. Before I can even ring the doorbell, the big brown front door opens and a knee-high girl with pigtails and bows tells me to go around to the backyard for her sister's party. I'm about to tell her that I'm here about Bert, but she closes the door before I can get the words out.

Batman and I walk to the backyard. There's cake, and more balloons and lots of little kids. Then my eyes lock on a man in the right corner, in tan pants and a tan shirt that reads MR. REPTILIAN. He's holding a turtle. Hope and possibility swirl through me.

Batman and I weave in and out of the minis who are darting, jumping, and hopping about the yard in no particular order. We inch closer to the man and the turtle. But before we can get to him, a woman in mom clothes approaches us.

"Can I help you?" she asks. Her shirt has a chocolate frosting smudge on the bottom. "Do you know my daughter?"

My words stick. All I see is the turtle. "I, um, don't. I knocked. And everyone was here, so I, um, came back. I lost my turtle."

Before the mom can say anything else, Pigtail Girl grabs my hand and leads me and Batman right to Mr. Reptilian.

45

A Smidgen of Hope

Batman is sniffing the air with purpose while I reach for the turtle. My turtle. But when Mr. Reptilian sets the shelled friend in my palm, I know it's not Bert. There's no heart-shaped mark on his shell. I swallow my heap of disappointment, hand the marching-over-to-me mom a flyer, and leave.

Batman and I move to the rest of the houses on the street. Knock and talk and hand out flyers. No one's seen Bert. But Mrs. Kaufman has a problem with the deer that keep eating her shrubs, Mr. Night's still waiting for the electrician who's an hour late, and Mrs. Henry has no hot water. When we run out of homes and mailboxes, I staple the rest of the flyers to the telephone poles along my path.

As Batman and I head back to Gramps's house, I hope Dillon and Charlie and Mom and Dad have had better luck.

I speed up. Maybe they found Bert. Maybe he's waiting for me. Quicker still. I hear my out-breaths. That's what my fourth-grade gym teacher used to call them. My sneakers slap the pavement as I run up the hill on Queens Drive. Hoping with all of me that they found him.

I swing open the front door. Gramps and Dillon and Mom and Dad and Charlie are sitting around the kitchen table. No Bert.

"Just because no one has seen him yet doesn't mean they won't," Dad says.

My heart slips and falls all the way to the linoleum tile floor. "Maybe he's back in the yard," I suggest, heading toward the screen door.

"I just checked," Gramps says.

"Me too," Dillon says.

I fall into a chair at the table and drop my head into my hands.

The doorbell rings. Dad looks at me. Then Mom. Then Dillon. Maybe the flyers are working.

Maybe someone found Bert.

Charlie runs to the door and opens it, and standing there are Ava, Sam, and Gracie.

"What are you guys doing here?" I ask.

"We just came from practice." It's Ava.

In that moment, I realize I forgot to stop by last night. I look for her mad to spill out, but it doesn't. She keeps talking. "Coach Aiden told us what's going on." Ava grabs my hands.

Pinwheels spin in my stomach.

"We're here to help," Gracie says, putting her short blond hair into a ponytail holder. Sam nods behind her.

"Well, no one's going anywhere without something to eat," Gramps says. He pulls a tomato, basil, and mozzarella salad from the counter, a bowl of tuna from the refrigerator, and a jumbo size bag of jalapeño potato chips from the pantry.

Over lunch, Dillon explains the routes we've already canvassed and suggests that some of us head to the farmers' market next.

I inhale my tuna, potato chip, and yellow mustard sandwich and go with my friends to the market. Mom takes Charlie home, Dad heads to the radio station to edit his interview of a guy who has created some robot that sniffs out disease, Dillon takes the next block, and Gramps stays back in case Bert returns.

"I'm sorry I didn't come by with Batman last night," I say to Ava. "With everything that happened with Bert, I honestly just forgot."

"It's okay. I tried out the Find Me sweater on Max the beagle."

"Did it work?"

"Almost. The code still needs some tweaking. But we're getting closer."

"That's great," I say.

"Thanks," Ava says. Then, "We'll find Bert."

"How can you be so sure?" I ask, unable to keep my worry from crawling over my words.

"I put it in the universe," she says.

I hug my friend.

Finally, she believes.

46

Lost or Found

Ava, Sam, Gracie, and I zigzag through the stands in the farmers' market. We're surrounded by pottery bowls, wind chimes, crystal necklaces, fruits, vegetables, nuts, and apples. Ava and Gracie are in charge of handing out the flyers, and Sam and I search the grass and the gravel path. The sun catches Sam's face, and her dark eyes shine. I hope they have the power to see the invisible. Or at least find Bert.

We weave and walk.

"I wish the Find Me sweater was working and Bert had one," Ava says. "Then we could use the app to locate him."

"I wish that, too," I say, grabbing my friend's hand.

"You guys hungry?" Eddie of Twin Oaks Farm asks as we walk by his stand. "Want some crisp, fresh McIntosh apples?"

"No, thanks," Ava says. "We're actually looking for Maggie's turtle, Bert. Any chance you've seen him?"

"A turtle? Nope." He takes a big bite out of one of the apples. "Sweet as candy. Sure I can't persuade you to take home a carton or two?"

"Thanks, but not today." Ava hands him a flyer.

"Cute fella. If I see him, I promise to call this number." Eddie turns to the woman coming up behind us with two little kids. "How would you and your crew like something that tastes sweet as sugar?"

As he's talking, I see leaves twitching on the extra heads of lettuce Eddie has lined up on the ground next to his table. I stop moving and stare.

There they go again. A slight wiggle. I tap Ava and point. She sees it, too.

Ava smiles. "That has to be Bert!" she says, squeezing my hand.

That smidgen of hope returns.

I breathe in all the crisp apple air around me, walk over to the right side of the table, and gently pull back the leaves.

Sitting there is not Bert.

It's a fat brown bunny with a mouth full of lettuce, who is now hopping away.

Disappointment rains down. We check the entire farmers' market. No Bert. My friends want to walk me home, but I don't want to go there yet. I text Dad and Mom, and they okay my new plan.

The girls and I split at LaGrange Street. I look under every bush I pass. Searching for Bert. My feet crunch the leaves on the path to Wade's Pond. I see a squirrel gathering acorns in her cheeks. I wonder if anyone told her she can't store *her* stuff.

"Sorry about Bert."

It's Mason.

"Thought you might be here," he says, picking up a flat pink stone.

Did he come here to see me?

I don't respond, because I'm not sure how. Truth is, I'm glad he's here.

He reaches out and hands me a piece of paper. When I look down, I see a cartoon drawing of Bert.

"Thanks," I say. "I really like it."

Then I see a squirrel dart up the tree. I point to her. "Do you think she's lost or found?"

"Hard to tell."

I think about Bert and wonder if anyone who sees him will even know he's lost. Mom told me I got lost at the beach when I was Charlie's age. She said she was so scared because in the sea of kids and families, no one would have known that I wasn't where I was supposed to be. Then I wonder what lost looks like.

"People should wear signs that say if they're lost," I say, thinking about Nana and the cherry slush. I let go of a brown stone, and it skims the top of the water.

"Nice one. Five skips." His takes three hops. "What if you didn't want to be found? Would you still need a sign?"

"I guess not." I pause, totally confused, and ask, "Who wouldn't want to be found?"

A breeze sweeps by. Followed by the squirrels. And a whole lot of air and space and quiet.

He shrugs.

I hand him the perfect skipping rock. He glides it across the water. Four hops. Then he says, "What if you don't even know you're lost?"

The thought of this pulls at my heart.

"Is it worse to know you're lost and be scared, or to not know you're lost and never find your way back?" I ask. Being afraid is bad, but maybe never finding your way home is worse.

"You're assuming the person who knows he's lost is scared, and the one who doesn't won't ever be found. Maybe neither of those things are true."

Maybe.

47

Dandelion Necklace

I hung the picture Mason drew of Bert next to the picture I did in art class of Izzie. They are the last things I see when I go to sleep and the first when I wake up. It's been four days since we lost Bert and almost four weeks since Izzie left. My sadness holds all the missing. I stare at the chart from my newest box.

Sticks. Today's toss. There are three: the nubby one I collected on a walk home with Charlie, the one I saved from the hike up Ridge Mountain when Ava and I got lost, and the one that looks like a wishbone, from Wade's Pond. I'm supposed to throw them out like leftover meatloaf. Like they're nothing. Like those times I picked them up never happened.

Then I remind myself what Dr. Sparrow said: Nana's brain wasn't healthy. Mine is. I won't forget. *Believe.*

I open my box, rub the threads of the white baby blanket, remove the sticks, and go downstairs to toss them in the parent-approved garbage.

Dad's waiting. I toss the sticks. They clang as they hit the metal bottom. I close the lid and go back upstairs to my room. The music of Jimmy Buffett's "Breathe In, Breathe Out, Move On" fills my bedroom.

When I open my door, Charlie's standing there with his hands behind his back.

"What are you doing here?" I ask.

"Waiting," he says.

"For what?"

"You. Mom said I'm not allowed in your room if the door's closed, so I was waiting here until you came out." He looks at me with his chocolate-brown eyes. "Are you done?" he asks.

I nod.

"This is for you." He hands me a dandelion necklace. "It's to make you happy. Like the necklace Ava got you. But less shiny and made of dandelions."

His kindness hugs me. I put on my flower necklace. "Thank you, Bear. I love it."

Then he runs his hand along the outer edge of the tub and says, "I know you're sad about Bert, but you don't have to worry about him."

"Why?" I ask, wondering if he knows something.

"Because I think he's with his bale."

"What does that mean?"

"Turtles hang in bales. He probably saw a friend and went to play, and will be back as soon as their game is over."

I nod, hoping he's right.

"Like me and Emma Rose." He pauses. "We're friends now." His smile shows off his missing tooth. "She let me play in her game of four square the other day. I even got to serve the first ball."

I look into his eyes and know that I will never forget him. He takes my hand and walks over to my bursting bookshelf. "Will you read to me?" he asks. We spend the next hour reading together. Our very own bale.

The ring of the phone startles me. Maybe it's about Bert.

I hear Dad's voice but can't make out his words. Then his footsteps find me. I stop reading. "Did someone find Bert?"

In the beat when he says nothing, I know the answer is no.

48

Just Believe

I rub my shoulder. It's sore from Batman sleeping on it all night long. I'm convinced he knows when I'm sad. Even with Charlie's dandelion necklace, the hole in my heart feels big. Now it's filled with Nana and Izzie and Bert. Batman makes this purring sound and slides his fluffy ball of a body as close to mine as he can and lies there until I feel better or move.

At today's practice, Dad reminds us the trap tournament is in two days. I turn to Ava. "I'm worried about leaving. What if Bert comes back?"

"The tournament is just for the day," she says.

"But it's all day. Morning until night."

"It's no different than you coming to practice," Sam says. "I mean, you're not sitting at home or at your grandfather's waiting for your turtle twenty-four hours a day."

Ava puts her arm around my shoulder. "Your gramps, mom, and brothers will be here if Bert comes back."

I know that's true. But it still feels weird leaving when something you love is missing.

"Besides, you'll feel better once we start singing on the ride there." Ava begins to hum. Loudly.

"You guys don't really do that, do you?" Mason says.

Gracie laughs. "It may be a thing that happens."

"Singing or not, we need you to win," Sam says to me. "You're the best on our squad. And I'm sick of losing at everything. It's not fair. My sister and I are part of the same genetic pool. How did I get all the loser genes?"

"Come on, Sam," I say. "Not winning in a trap tournament doesn't mean you're a loser." My heart hurts for her. I've seen the trophy room at her house. It's filled with best this and all-around-greatest that. Some trophies are glass, others are tall and shiny in silver or gold. They all have her sister's name engraved on them.

When I get home from practice, Batman and I walk to Gramps's house.

"Do you think Bert is coming back?" I ask Gramps. He's leaning over the garden, pulling the weeds. I know he'll be honest. When I had to get a shot at the doctor, he was the only one who told me it would hurt. And he was right. It did. A lot.

"Of course he's coming back," he says with an assurance that surprises me.

"Have you seen him?" I look around the yard, hoping maybe he's in the back corner, eating a big, fat worm.

"Nope. Haven't seen him."

I deflate.

"Just believe. That's all," he says.

Is the universe even listening?

"Is believing in something really enough?"

"Sometimes it has to be. Sometimes believing in something is all we have." He straightens up and stares at me with his crystal-blue eyes. "Just have faith and give him time." He rubs his back with his hands, then says, "Fill the feeder for me, will you?"

Feeding the birds was another one of Nana's jobs. I pluck the fish-shaped ceramic feeder off the tree and fill it with seed. I'm not sure why this bird feeder is shaped like a fish, but Nana loved it.

Batman digs up a tennis ball and drops the chewed-up, dirt-covered thing at my feet. I hang up the full feeder, toss him the ball, and watch Batman and the birds come back for more. I wish it was that easy with Bert.

I weed until the vegetable bed's clear, then hug my grandfather good-bye and hope I can believe the way he does.

On the way home, I stop by the pond. I have something I need to do. I find a flat pink rock, make a wish, tell the universe, cross my fingers, and believe.

Then I send the rock sailing across the pond.

Four hops.

49

One Day

After school the next day, I meet with Dr. Sparrow. I don't see my waiting-room friend. There's a boy with a buzz cut reading, and a girl across from him sitting with a person who looks like her mom. They have the same bouncy brown curls.

When I'm called in for my appointment, I go in alone. Dad stays in the waiting room.

Dr. Sparrow's wearing a neon-green shirt that says ANYTHING IS POSSIBLE.

I tell Dr. Sparrow about Lost Bert. And how it feels like so many of the things I love leave.

"It's hard when the pets and people we love aren't with us anymore," she says. "It's okay to feel sad."

I grab a tissue and hand her one of my charts.

STUFF	RATE	TOSSED	REWARD EARNED
3 milk cartons	5-worried to toss	X	10 points
5 Blue Bonnet gum wrappers	1-can toss, but not happy	X	2 points
3 bendy straws	2-can toss, but less happy	X	4 points
6 rocks	3-will toss, but hurts	X	6 points
3 sticks	4-don't want to toss	X	8 points
gecko necklace from Nana	10+-never tossing		infinity points
tassel from Nana's favorite scarf	8-can't let go		16 points
2 napkins	2-can toss, but less happy	X	4 points
yellow baby sock	9-hurts my heart to toss		18 points
2 butterscotch candy wrappers	5-worried to toss	X	10 points
diaper tabs	6-nervous to toss		12 points
piece from disposable bottle	6-nervous to toss		12 points
baby hair	9-hurts my heart to toss		18 points
button from Bud the Bear	9-hurts my heart to toss		18 points
yellow plastic fork and fireworks plate	3-will toss, but hurts	X	6 points
binkie with green frog	7-scared to toss		14 points
photos of Izzie	10+-never tossing		infinity points
threads from baby blanket	8-can't let go		16 points

"You're showing tremendous improvement," she says.

I know that's true. Many of my things now live in the metal trash bin. And my charts have lots of *X*'s.

"It's getting easier to throw some things in the garbage," I say. "Though there are still times I worry I'll forget."

"That can happen. But you're learning to let go."

A small smile slips out.

"Before you came here today," she says, "your parents contacted me."

"Why?"

"Rita had inquired about another foster baby who needed a short-term home."

Excitement ripples through my body. "What did they say?"

She clears her throat. "They're still worried fostering would be too stressful, and they don't want to disrupt all the good progress you've made."

"So, no baby?" The excitement drains onto the floor of the office.

"Not now, Maggie. But I told your parents that this is something that could be good for all of you again."

"Thanks," I say. Then add, "I get it now. Why we do it. That it's an important job. That it's not about being remembered. But about loving these tiny humans. Because we can."

When I return home, Charlie and I make cards for Bert. There's lots of glitter and markers and feathers. I'm not sure why feathers, but Charlie insists that Bert loves brown and white and pink feathers.

I run my fingers along the feathers but don't put one in my pocket. I'm trying, even though trying is really hard.

"What are you guys doing?" Dillon asks.

"Making cards for Bert," Charlie says.

"Why?" Dillon bounces a basketball as he waits for one of us to explain.

"Because it's fun and it'll make Bert happy when he comes home," Charlie says like it's obvious. "Want to make him a card?"

Dillon drops the ball and joins us.

Maybe this is what believing looks like.

The three of us glue, glitter, and draw until we're covered with red and blue and gold sparkles and neon splashes of marker.

We tape the cards for Bert to his plastic tub. Charlie hugs my middle and tells me he's going to build a Lego tower for when Bert comes home.

I follow Dillon to his room. There are two huge posters on his wall, one of Larry Bird and the other of Paul Pierce.

"You'll watch for Bert while I'm at the tournament tomorrow?" I ask.

He nods. "I'm sorry, Maggie. I know this is all my fault."

"I'm sad about Bert," I say. "But I'm not mad at you anymore." I slide next to my big brother.

I remember when I was in fourth grade and went to Mayflower Beach with Ava's family for the day. I wanted to bring the headphones Dillon got from Nana and Gramps for his birthday. But he said I couldn't. So I secretly borrowed them. Thinking I'd put them back before he'd even notice they were gone. But at the beach, I fell asleep. High tide came in, and the headphones washed into the ocean. Along with my flip-flops.

I felt all kinds of awful.

Dillon was mad. At first, supermad.

But then one day, he wasn't mad anymore. He was just my big brother again.

I leave Dillon and go to my room to get my trap bag ready for the tournament tomorrow. I hear the rain pelting against my window. I finish packing and settle next to one of my boxes. I hold Bert's rock and rub the threads of Izzie's blanket with my fingers. I try and remember each day that I got to be a small part of their big world. I prepare a speech in my head that I'm going to deliver to my parents about another foster baby. About me getting better. About having a heart big enough to love a lot and brain healthy enough to let go.

But then Mom knocks on my door. She hugs me tight, tells me how proud she is of me, and promises to keep looking for Bert while I'm at the tournament.

I swallow my speech. And hope the disappearance of my big, scary mad, and my emptier boxes will make them change their mind.

One day.

50

Girl Power

The rain has stopped, but the air is thick when I get into the van on Saturday morning. Ava's already there. "Saved you a seat." She pats the space next to her.

"Your patch looks great," I tell her.

"Thanks." She smiles at her yellow-and-red patch that says AA-25 STRAIGHT. "I love that we have matching patches now."

"Me too," I say.

Sam leans over the seat in front of us with a handful of gummy worms. "Want some?"

Ava shakes her head no, and I take three red ones.

"Before I left the house this morning," Sam says, "my dad told me that he thought we might be able to win the whole tournament."

"Cool. Is he coming to watch?" I ask.

Sam shakes her head.

The whole time we've been on the team together, I've seen her parents only once. It was our first shoot. And we lost. They haven't been back since.

"My sister's running in her cross-country team's final competition for the season," she says.

"It's *your* final competition, too," Ava says.

I shoot her a look.

"What? It's true," she says.

I lean in close to Ava and whisper, "Just because it's true doesn't mean it's helpful." I nod toward Sam, who's wiping the tears running down her cheeks. I move into the seat next to Sam and offer her my earbuds. "Thanks," she says as she slides them on and opens her playlist.

Gracie's reading, and Mason's in a seat by himself in the back of the van. When I glance over, he nods. I don't know what happened with his dad, but I'm glad he's here.

The road's bumpy, and my good-luck pancakes from this morning feel like they could turn into bad-luck throw-up. After about ten minutes, Ava breaks into song. Sam ignores her. But when Mason belts out the chorus, everyone laughs. And we all join in.

About an hour into the ride to the tournament, I dig out my Go On, Change the World! notebook from my bag and start to sketch. I draw Nana's face and the just-because present she gave me.

"Hey, that looks like the gecko necklace you used to wear," Sam says.

The one I keep. In my box.

It takes about two hours, two bathroom stops, and one burrito lunch break to get to Braiden Shooting Club, where the tournament's being held. The dirt road is narrow and winding as it bends along the tall trees. Dad parks the van, and we all pour out. The sun shines on the row of team canopy tents that line the parking lot at the edge of the two main shooting ranges. Dad sets up our tent. It's green and says EAGLE EYES OF FISH, FUR, AND FLY in yellow letters across the front. Then he goes into the cabin to register our team. When he comes out with our tournament T-shirts, we're sitting in a circle under our tent playing hot potato with Mason's soccer ball. Ava and Sam are out. Just me, Gracie, and Mason are left. Dad tells us there are eighty kids registered. Twelve teams. Only seven girls in all. And we are four of them.

All I think is, *Girl Power.*

I head to the bathroom in the cabin at the Braiden Club. In the stall, I see that someone has written *ES loves JS*, and I wonder where they are now. I imagine them in love on a beach at sunset somewhere. Graffiti covers the entire door. *Sofia was here. Jordan rules. I love trap.*

When I leave the bathroom, I see Sam on the phone. I wave, but she doesn't notice me.

I walk over to her. She's nodding and wrapping her black hair tightly around her pointer finger but saying nothing. Then she hangs up and looks at me.

"He'll never be proud of me."

"That's not true," I say.

I grab her hand, walk out of the building, into

the woods, and find a stump tucked between two huge oak trees for us to sit on.

"You should have heard him going on and on about my sister," Sam says. "How she won the whole meet. How she's so fast. How she's the best. I could feel his pride oozing through the stupid phone." She pauses. "I love my sister. But I don't get why he can't be proud of both of us."

"I'm sure he is," I say.

She shakes her head. "Winning is the only thing he understands. The only way he'll ever be proud of me."

I hug my friend. We sit until her tears stop. Then we leave our spot in the woods and head back to the team. As we pass all the brightly colored canopies, I see Dad waving us into the squad huddle.

"Okay, we're all here now," he says. "I want you to be the best trapshooters you can be out there today."

I think of Sam.

"Believe in yourselves. Be good sports to your squadmates and the other teams."

Across the huddle, Mason's eyes fall on me.

Dad finishes with a "Fight hard!"

All hands meet in the middle of our circle. Together we yell, "Let's go!"

The circle disbands. Ava and Gracie start talking about the Clay Birds' best shooter, some kid named George.

Sam wanders away from the group.

I follow her. "You okay?"

She shrugs, then stares at me with serious eyes. "Can I tell you a secret?"

"Always," I say.

"This is a cross-your-heart kind of secret."

I nod.

Sam leans in close. "I switched the shells," she whispers, biting her lip.

This was not the kind of secret I thought she was going to share. "What do you mean?"

She inches even closer. "I swapped the steel shells for lead ones."

"How?"

"I snuck the lead shells into the steel-shell box."

The air slowly leaks out of my lungs.

"Why?" I ask.

"Think about it, Maggie. If I use the lead shells, I have a real chance of winning."

"You can't do that, Sam."

"The shells are already in the box," she says, "ready to go."

"But those lead shells are banned here, just like at our club. They can poison the environment and turtles like Bert."

Sam puts her head on my shoulder. "Maggie, I would never do it if Bert was anywhere near here. I promise. But he's not. And no one will ever know I switched them."

"I'll know," I say, nervous creeping up my back.

"But you promised to keep my secret." Sam grabs my hands.

My stomach twists.

"Maggie, please. I just want him to be proud of me. One time," Sam says.

I think about Dad and how lucky I am to have that feeling all the time. Then I promise to keep my friend's secret.

51

A Big Fat Mistake

"You're the best," Sam says, hugging me tight.

We head back to the Eagle Eyes canopy.

"I need some volunteers to grab the rest of the waters from the back of the van," Dad says to the group.

"I'll go," I say.

"Me too." It's Mason.

On the way there, I leap over a puddle, stumble, and land, *splat*, in the water. The murky mix splashes all over my legs. As I lift my muddy boot from the water, I see a small turtle. Like Bert, but without the heart-shaped spot. I bend down. I miss my shelled friend. Wonder where he is. Then I wonder about this fella. Sam said she'd never do anything that would hurt Bert, but what about all the animals like Bert? What will Sam's lead shells do to their homes?

As I think of all the turtles and fish and frogs that live out here, my brain spins. And deep down in the place that knows my truths, I realize I've made a mistake.

A big fat mistake.

"You all right?" Mason asks.

"Yeah," I say. "Why?"

"You got crazy pale all of a sudden. The only time that ever happened to me, I fainted."

I point to the turtle. "I just miss Bert."

Almost the whole truth.

When we get to the van, I ask him, "What would you do if someone told you a secret that if you shared, could hurt a friend? But if you didn't, other bad things could happen."

"For real? Or is this from that Litmus game you told me about? I'm only on level three," he says.

"It's not from Litmus."

This is about Sam. But I can't say that.

"Did you promise you wouldn't tell?"

I nod.

"Then you can't say anything. Or you'll be breaking a promise."

I know that's true. But I wonder if keeping *this* secret is worse than breaking a promise.

When we get back with the waters, Dad says we have some time before the kickoff meeting. I leave the group and find a big, flat rock to sit on, away from everyone else. My brain is filled with things that don't make sense. I take out my phone and call the only other person I need to talk to.

"I thought you'd be on the range already," Gramps says. The familiar rhythm of his voice feels like Nana's blue afghan.

"Soon. The teams are still registering."

"Oh."

"Any Bert sightings?" Figure I might as well ask while we're talking.

"Nope, but have faith. He'll come back."

I wonder how Gramps can still be so sure of this. Of anything.

"How's the garden?" I know I'm procrastinating, but I don't know how to start.

"You called me from your tournament to ask me about the garden that you helped me weed yesterday?"

"Well, there's this other thing," I say.

"Listening."

I tell Gramps about Sam's secret and my promise.

He's silent.

That can't be good. He's never quiet.

"You need to tell your dad."

"The coach of our squad?"

"Yep, that's the one."

I hang up my phone and head back to the team. Gramps is right. I need to do something. Talk to someone. But he's wrong about who.

When I find Sam, she's under the team tent, playing Litmus on her phone. I tap her shoulder. "We need to talk."

I move to a space empty of trapshooters, and Sam follows.

"I've changed my mind. You can't use the lead shells," I whisper. "It's wrong."

Her hands fly to her hips, and in a voice splashed with anger, she says, "It's not wrong! It's not even a big deal."

"It *is* a big deal! They're banned for a reason. Animals could get hurt."

"Maggie, nothing bad is going to happen."

"But it could," I say, filled with worry.

"But it won't."

"You don't know that."

She stares at me for a long minute. "What are you going to do? Run and tell your dad?"

I don't answer.

"You can't go back on your word," she says.

"I'm begging you to do the right thing, Sam."

"And I'm begging you to keep your promise, Maggie. You're supposed to be my friend."

52

Consequences

My insides dip and dive. I don't know what to do.

I think of Bert.

The puddle turtle.

Sam.

Her dad.

My dad.

"Twenty minutes to the start, everyone," Dad calls to the group. Then he pats my shoulder and smiles.

I look at him and my confusion finds a path. I wait until the squad disperses, and quietly, ask him to take a walk with me.

Dad and I move past the coaches with hot coffee, the gray cabin, and the oak trees on the path. We keep going. I don't want to run into anyone. We wind around to the left and onto an empty trail in the woods.

"Dad, what I'm going to tell you is between us. You and me. Not me and Coach."

He looks confused.

"I need my dad right now, not my coach."

"Okay." He sits next to me on a tree stump. "What's going on?" His eyes search mine for answers.

When all the words are out, the air is filled with broken promises.

Dad lifts my chin and looks into my eyes. "I'm proud of you for telling me."

"What's going to happen to Sam?"

"I'm not entirely sure of all the consequences, but I do know she won't be participating in today's tournament."

My breath sticks in my throat. "Dad, please don't do that. Just tell her not to use the lead shells. The tournament hasn't even started yet."

"The rules are clear, Maggie. What Sam did is a serious violation."

"I wouldn't have told you if I knew you were

going to kick her out of the tournament," I say. "Just talk to her. Please! Or pick a different punishment."

"Maggie, you did the right thing even if the consequences aren't what you thought they'd be."

"She'll hate me," I say.

"It's going to be okay, Maggie." Dad kisses my forehead. "But we need to get back."

"I'll meet you over there." I think about Bert, Izzie, and Sam. And the swarm of feelings buzzing in my brain.

I'm still sitting on the stump when Dad's text comes through about an emergency squad meeting. The kickoff safety meeting is about to start, and the groups are moving into the fenced-in area. Dad and my squad are at our canopy. Well, my sort-of squad.

It's Mason and Ava and Gracie.

Sam is missing.

"There's been a change in the plan for the day," Dad says. "Sam's not going to be joining us."

I swallow hard.

Ava looks at me. Eyes wide. I say nothing. I know why Sam's leaving. And I know what she did was wrong. But her leaving still feels bad.

"Luckily," Dad says, "Belle was here today, registered and shooting for one of the other Eagle Eyes squads. She's graciously agreed to shoot, instead, with our squad. We've made the necessary changes at registration. We compete shortly, so gather your things and head over to the kickoff meeting."

"Wait, where's Sam?" Ava asks.

"She violated team rules, and her mom is on her way to pick her up."

"Her mom's coming to the tournament now?" Gracie says.

Dad nods.

"What did she do?" Ava asks.

"She made a mistake. And there are consequences."

"What kind of mistake?"

"The details aren't important right now," Dad says. "We need to regroup and head out."

At that moment, I see Belle walking toward our tent and give her a grateful-for-you hug. Then I notice Dad talking to a linebacker-size man with a bushy beard, wearing a Bruins cap.

Mason's father is here.

53

Find My Way

Our squad, which feels nothing like *our* squad, is called. I hear Ava tell Belle that the Clay Birds are in the lead.

We take our places.

As squad leader, I step into position one. Mason follows, in two, then Ava, Gracie, and Belle. The scorer, in a neon-yellow shirt, sitting in a high wooden chair, nods that he's ready. I look at my squad. They're ready.

"Pull!" I call.

The neon-orange clay disc sails into the air, and with it comes a million sorries to Sam and a missing filled with forever good-byes. I try to focus, but the tears roll down my cheeks and all I see is the cloudy watercolor of a disc. The disc crashes to the ground.

I take a deep breath. I have to do better. For me. For Sam. For my squad.

When it's my turn again, I reposition my feet. *Start at the beginning. Left foot in front of right, feed the shell into the side, click the black button underneath.* I lift my gun, square it on my shoulder, then lean in. "Pull!" I yell a second time.

Let the snowman be your guide.

I see the disc. It's mine. I release the trigger and watch as the sky fills with a million tiny pieces of neon orange.

I find my way.

We all find our way.

It's a long day. When all the squads finish, we wait while the officials calculate the scores. Then a man in a navy shirt and khaki pants announces there needs to be a shootoff. Two players are tied for second place.

I cross my toes, and Ava squeezes my hand.

Khaki Pants says, "Can Maggie Hunt and George

Taylor come to field two?" And I feel Dad's arms wrap around me.

I step up to the field. George is from Clay Birds. We need to shoot until someone misses.

I go first. Hit the clay pigeon. Orange rain.

George does the same.

This goes on for ten shots. And then we're told to move back ten feet and begin again.

"Pull!" I watch the bird, pull the trigger, and the wind sweeps in from the right.

"Loss," Khaki Pants yells from his high chair.

"Pull!" George calls. I watch him focus and shoot. The disc shatters. His squad erupts in loud cheers.

Our squad takes second place, and I take third in the individuals. As I walk over to the circle of picnic tables where the awards will be handed out, I see Mason at the food table, digging into the chip bowl.

"Hey," I say, grabbing a handful of barbecue potato chips.

"Hi," he says. "You were, um, I mean, you shot amazing today."

"Thanks." I feel the heat pepper my face and

neck. "Is that your dad?" I ask, pointing to the man walking toward us wearing a Bruins cap.

"Yep. He came to see the best almost-all-girl trapshooting team."

"What changed?" I ask.

"I made burgers last night with fried eggs and lots of hot sauce. Just like the ones from Burger Shack."

I smile.

"And your dad came by," he says.

"Your house?" I ask. I didn't even know Dad knew where Mason lived.

He nods. "Your dad and my dad talked for a while, and then my dad and I talked. For the first time in maybe forever. I told him that I want him to be a part of *my* life. And that includes trap." He exhales. "It was a start."

"A really good start," I say.

54

Did You Know?

On the ride home, I sit with Ava. I overhear Gracie leaving a message for Sam. Then another. But Sam's not answering. Confusion bleeds through the van. They still don't know what happened. I do, but won't say anything. This is Sam's story to tell. Mason's across the aisle from me. This time no one sings, even though we came in second. Our medals are on the seat next to Dad, who's called a squad meeting for later this week. For now, however, he said we should enjoy our success.

When we pull into the parking lot, it's late. The bright lights drape across the dark lot. After all the members of my squad are picked up, Dad and I get into his truck. I put my trap bag in the back, and Dad leans over and says, "Great job today, Maggie."

"Thanks."

"I'm not just talking about trap." He looks at me. "You did the right thing even when the right thing was hard to do."

We listen to *The Best of Bob Dylan*. I stare out the window at the moon. I wonder if Izzie and Bert see it.

When we walk in the front door, Mom hugs me first. She's smiling. I know Dad told her what I did. And that our team came in second and I came in third.

Then Charlie comes in. Eyes big and bright. He squeezes me hard. "Did you know that one time in London they found a hamster and a cat and a dinosaur on the train?" Then he adds, "The dinosaur was the blow-up kind, but the others were real."

"No, I can honestly say that I didn't know."

Then Dillon comes in. He's carrying something. "Did you know that one time in the town of Maker

on Brookville Drive they found a turtle in a puddle?" he asks.

Then from behind his back he pulls a turtle with
a bright-orange belly and a heart-shaped spot on
his shell.

55

Forever Pet

My happiness bursts from the bottoms of my feet. "Bert!" I hug my forever pet. "How did you find him? Where did you find him?"

"You're never going to believe it. You know the woman who lives in the spooky ranch with the crooked black shutters, the house we always skip on Halloween?" Dillon asks.

I nod.

"*She* found Bert!"

I remember talking to her. She was the one who said he could get run over, shell and all.

"Where?"

"In her yard in a puddle that was left over from the rain last night," Dillon says.

"She recognized the heart-shaped marking from the missing-turtle flyer and called the number on it," Mom says.

"We found him, Maggie!" Charlie says, dancing in a circle around Bert.

"You're the best finder," I say to my little brother.

"Izzie is still gone, though," he adds.

"I know, Bear. But you're here."

That's when I know we're all exactly where we belong.

After a celebration filled with banana ice cream, hot fudge, and whipped cream, I take Bert upstairs to my room. When I put him in his plastic tub, he looks happy to be home.

I hang with him awhile, then wash my hands and close my bedroom door. I text Sam for the fifth time. When she doesn't respond again, I reluctantly take out a box. My pockets are empty, but I need to toss another item on my chart. Today, it's something from my newest box. A number seven, the frog binkie.

I move around the threads and the photo album and lay the binkie on my lap. My mind trails back to one afternoon with Izzie. I was studying for my math test and Izzie wouldn't stop crying until I gave her this binkie with the green frog and rocked her gently. I squeeze the binkie.

Batman sits next to me. He sniffs the floor, the box, and the binkie. Then mouths the binkie with the green frog.

"Drop it," I say. "You can't help me with this, Batman." He spits out the binkie and licks my face.

Together we leave my room and walk down to the garbage can of parent-inspected, doctor-ordered trash.

I hold Izzie's binkie in my hand for an extralong beat and then toss it into the metal can.

I should feel proud. That's what Dr. Sparrow says. I wait for the feeling to come, but it doesn't. I go upstairs and peek into the room that was Izzie's. I decide my pride might be stuck behind my missing. I leave the empty room and visit with Bert, who's happily resting on his rock.

STUFF	RATE	TOSSED	REWARD EARNED
3 milk cartons	5-worried to toss	X	10 points
5 Blue Bonnet gum wrappers	1-can toss, but not happy	X	2 points
3 bendy straws	2-can toss, but less happy	X	4 points
6 rocks	3-will toss, but hurts	X	6 points
3 sticks	4-don't want to toss	X	8 points
gecko necklace from Nana	10+-never tossing		infinity points
tassel from Nana's favorite scarf	8-can't let go		16 points
2 napkins	2-can toss, but less happy	X	4 points
yellow baby sock	9-hurts my heart to toss		18 points
2 butterscotch candy wrappers	5-worried to toss	X	10 points
diaper tabs	6-nervous to toss		12 points
piece from disposable bottle	6-nervous to toss	X	12 points
baby hair	9-hurts my heart to toss		18 points
button from Bud the Bear	9-hurts my heart to toss		18 points
yellow plastic fork and fireworks plate	3-will toss, but hurts	X	6 points
binkie with green frog	7-scared to toss	X	14 points
photos of Izzie	10+-never tossing		infinity points
threads from baby blanket	8-can't let go		16 points

"What do you think he did on his big adventure?" Dillon asks, coming into my room.

"I bet he went to the zoo and played with other turtles," Charlie says, joining us around the tub. "Maybe he made a new friend."

"That's people, Bear," Dillon says.

"Maybe he made a friend," Charlie says.

"Maybe he did, Bear," I say, scooping up my little brother and putting him in my lap.

Just like that, the missing goes away.

And then I feel it.

A tiny speck of proud.

56

Just a Box

Over the next six months, there are lots of changes that make me feel all the feels. Sam comes to trap practice and tells the squad what happened. She's on probation for now, but Dad announces he'll reevaluate next season. She apologizes to everyone. Well, almost everyone. She's still mad at me. Ava thinks Sam just needs time. But I'm not so sure. She refuses to answer my texts or phone calls and won't sit at our lunch table anymore. It makes me supersad inside, but I know in my heart of truths that telling Dad was the right thing to do. Ava agrees. So does Belle. But Gracie isn't totally convinced. She sits with Sam at lunch. I broke a promise. And that's a big thing.

My Go On, Change the World! notebook has a page that just says:

1. *Believe.*
2. *Love.*
3. *Let go.*

Gramps and I plant two small blueberry bushes. One for Nana and one for Izzie.

Mom and I go to school and finish cleaning out my locker. Together. And each one of my boxes empties. A little at a time until they're just a bunch of boxes. Eleven empty boxes. One empty locker. Twelve charts full of X's.

STUFF	RATE	TOSSED	REWARD EARNED
3 milk cartons	5-worried to toss	X	10 points
5 Blue Bonnet gum wrappers	1-can toss, but not happy	X	2 points
3 bendy straws	2-can toss, but less happy	X	4 points
6 rocks	3-will toss, but hurts	X	6 points
3 sticks	4-don't want to toss	X	8 points
gecko necklace from Nana	10+-never tossing	can keep	infinity points

STUFF	RATE	TOSSED	REWARD EARNED
tassel from Nana's favorite scarf	8-can't let go	X	16 points
2 napkins	2-can toss, but less happy	X	4 points
yellow baby sock	9-hurts my heart to toss	X	18 points
2 butterscotch candy wrappers	5-worried to toss	X	10 points
diaper tabs	6-nervous to toss	X	12 points
piece from disposable bottle	6-nervous to toss	X	12 points
baby hair	9-hurts my heart to toss	X	18 points
button from Bud the Bear	9-hurts my heart to toss	X	18 points
yellow plastic fork and fireworks plate	3-will toss, but hurts	X	6 points
binkie with green frog	7-scared to toss	X	14 points
photos of Izzie	10+-never tossing	can keep	infinity points
threads from baby blanket	8-can't let go	X	16 points

Dr. Sparrow says I'm allowed to keep my photos of Izzie in my Remember Me album and my gecko necklace. As for the rest, it's gone, and Dr. Sparrow was right. My mind helps my heart remember the things that are important.

At today's session, she reminds me that Cipher may come back and tells me what to do if I get those worried, I-can't-let-go feelings again. We make a list together and put it in my Go On, Change the World! notebook.

1. Talk back to Cipher.
2. Make a chart.
3. Rate your stuff from 1 to 10.
4. Toss it.
5. Move on.
6. Sketch.
7. Listen to music.

After my appointment with Dr. Sparrow, I ride my bike to Ava's. She tells me the coding club finally got the Find Me sweater to work and hands me a green one for Bert and blue one for Batman.

I hug my best friend and then tell her everything. She promises to help if Cipher returns. I add her to my list.

8. Talk to Ava.

That night, I'm tucked under Nana's blue afghan, playing Litmus with Mom, Dad, Dillon, and Charlie.

The doorbell rings.

I open our bright-blue door, and standing there is Rita, holding baby #2.

I now know I don't need things to remember people or places or feelings. I have a healthy brain and a big heart.

Maggie's Playlist

Alabama Shakes—"I Found You"

Grace Potter—"Timekeeper"

Carole King—"Up on the Roof"

Train—"Calling All Angels"

Indigo Girls—"Closer to Fine"

Bob Dylan—"Blowin' in the Wind"

Marvin Gaye—"Mercy Mercy Me"

Bob Dylan—"Mr. Tambourine Man"

Julia Brennan—"Inner Demons"

Counting Crows—"You Can't Count On Me"

Jimmy Buffett—"Breathe In, Breathe Out,
Move On"

A Note on Hoarding in Children from Dr. Kathleen Trainor, Clinical Psychologist

Many children like to collect items of interest—for example, stuffed animals, rocks, seashells, or Matchbox cars. Children who hoard collect things randomly that objectively seem to have little or no value. This may include candy wrappers, food containers, used straws, broken toys, or clothes that no longer fit—items that to an objective observer can look like garbage. These children have a very strong emotional attachment to these saved things. In addition, they often worry excessively about their hoarded items, for fear they may be gone.

Children who hoard usually keep their hoarded items in their room in a special place and frequently need to check to make sure they are all there. It often feels like these saved things are so important that they have feelings and to throw them away would be "killing" them. Children's anxiety about their hoarded items can be so excessive that it can interfere with their functioning. The thought that anyone would throw any of these things away can cause them to panic and become very angry and upset.

There is not a lot of research about children who hoard, but cognitive behavioral therapy, which involves encouraging the child to work in a step-by-step manner to throw away their hoarded items and manage their anxious feelings, has been shown to be an effective approach to help these children.

Author's Note

In the story, Maggie is part of a trapshooting team. For those who may not be familiar with trap, it's a sport where participants use a shotgun to break saucer-shaped clay discs thrown into the air from a spring device called a trap machine. Trapshooting is a sport that has long been a part of the Olympic Games.

Experts Consulted

Hoarding in Children

Dr. Kathleen Trainor, founder of the Trainor Center in Natick, Massachusetts, has treated children and adolescents with anxiety-based disorders using the latest in evidence-based approaches for more than thirty years. Her practice, which focuses on Cognitive Behavioral Therapy (CBT), is tailored to meet each child's needs. A senior psychologist on the staff of the Child Psychiatry Clinic at Massachusetts General Hospital, Dr. Trainor holds a Master's Degree in social work and a Doctorate in clinical psychology. She has been on the faculty of Harvard Medical School for more than twenty-five years.

Since 1988, she has been a private practice psychotherapist, providing adult, adolescent, couple, and family CBT in solo practice as a licensed independent certified social worker (LICSW) and then as a licensed psychologist. Dr. Trainor presents to professional and community groups in the areas of Cognitive Behavioral Treatment of Anxiety Disorders, Obsessive-Compulsive Disorder, Tourette's syndrome, Autism, Trichotillomania, and more. She also provides training and consultations to schools and therapists in various clinical settings.

She is known for her unique and widely used 7-Step TRAINOR Method featured in her book, *Calming Your Anxious Child: Words to Say and Things to Do.*

Adoption and Short-Term Foster Care

Amy S. Cohen, LICSW, Executive Director of Adoptions With Love (AWL), has more than thirty-one years of experience working in the field of adoption, along with a Bachelor's Degree in psychology and a Master's Degree in social work. She has been working at AWL since 1986, and she became Executive Director in October 2001.

Cohen works extensively with expectant birth

parents over the phone and in person. She also conducts home studies and provides postplacement services for adoptive families. She is married and has two adult children and a grandson.

Eastern Painted Turtle Information

Greg Mertz, DVM, has treated or presided over the care of one hundred thousand wild animals. He started his career as a research assistant in an anthracite coal research laboratory in University Park, Pennsylvania. His passion for life sciences education led him to become a veterinarian.

Mertz is now Chief Executive Officer of the New England Wildlife Center (NEWC), where he combines his skills in veterinary medicine with his interest in natural history and wildlife biology. It was his idea to build NEWC's Thomas E. Curtis Wildlife Hospital and Education Center. He also serves as the Odd Pet Vet, running NEWC's fee-for-service commercial veterinary practice, which he founded in 1995. He treats about one hundred species of animals, including chickens, pigeons, parrots, degus, rabbits, guinea pigs, rats, mice, hamsters, all manner of snakes, lizards, and turtles, and invertebrates like hermit crabs, cockroaches, tarantulas, millipedes, and scorpions. One hundred percent of funds earned help fund the work of NEWC.

Mertz writes a column for the *Pet Gazette* and has produced and hosted more than 150 episodes of *New England's Wild Legacy*, a cable access television program.

Mertz has been on the teaching staff of Mount Ida College, Dowling College, the National Museum of Natural History at the Smithsonian, and the Cummings School of Veterinary Medicine at Tufts University. He also designed and wrote the curricula for the Sevens and As Clear As Mud educational programs that are presented by NEWC and used by many of Boston's and surrounding communities' elementary and middle schools. In addition Greg is the lead veterinarian for the Museum of Science in Boston and Mass Audubon's Drumlin Farm Wildlife Sanctuary.

Acknowledgments

This story centers around holding things in your heart that are important to you. Thankfully, my heart is full. Of love. Of memories. Of people who mean everything to me. Topping that list is my family.

James, there is no one I want to share this wonderful life with more than you. You are my best friend and the love of my life. Thank you for always being by my side. For loving me so completely. And for being you.

Joshua and Gregory, I am so proud and grateful and happy to be your mom. You bring love and light and laughter to my world and my heart every day. Love you huge!

Dad and Sandy and Gia, there are no more triumphant champions of my books and my family and me than you three. How lucky I am to have you leading the way. Love you.

To my brothers and sisters, nieces and nephews,

love you so much. And to Rena, hugs and thanks and hats off for coming up with the title. And to Joan, for believing after only the first twenty pages that this story should be told.

To Joy Peskin, my deepest gratitude. Thank you for your editorial input, for loving Maggie, and for believing in my ability to tell her story. And to Elizabeth Lee, Lindsay Wagner, Kelsey Marrujo, Lucy Del Priore, Katie Halata, Madison Furr, and #TeamGiveandTake, a huge and heartfelt thank-you for all your hard work in bringing this book into the world. Grateful to be part of the FSG family.

Andrea Cascardi, thank you for believing in me. I am grateful for your insight, your input, and your guidance. Excited to be working together. I can't wait to see where our path leads.

Trish Lawrence, thank you for helping me bring Maggie's story to readers, and for encouraging me to be the best writer I can be. And for my EMLA family, may all your books always grace the shelves.

Anna Kontos, a forever thanks and love for all your help with the curriculum guides, the story, and life.

A huge thanks to Rayna Fredman for all the

book love, friendship, and help with the curriculum guide.

To my early readers—Joan Siff, Reesa Fischer, Sarah Aronson, Katrina Knudson, Victoria Coe, Sarah Azibo, Sophie McKibben—I am most thankful for your kindness, input, guidance, and friendship.

Joshua and Sophie, I'm most grateful for the podcast insight, inspiration, and input. And, Gregory, thank you huge for the brainstorming sessions, feedback, and story guidance.

Dr. Kathleen Trainor, Maggie could not have been brought to life without your insight, knowledge, and expertise. You are gracious and wise. Thank you!

Dr. Armin Lilienfeld, thank you for your thoughts on the issue of dementia, and how it might present in Maggie's world. Most grateful for your feedback.

To the Hot Shots team of Fin Fur and Feather in Millis, Massachusetts, a huge thanks for teaching me how to shoot trap and allowing me to learn alongside all of you. To Taylor, Deb, and George Connors, a special thanks for introducing me to the world of trap. You're a very special family, and I so appreciate all your help.

Amy Cohen, I am most grateful for you and the time taken to educate me about adoptions and foster care in Massachusetts. You do so much for so many every day. Thank you!

Jamie Grossman and Dana, my heart is full. Thank you for taking the time to meet with me and for sharing your stories and your love for babies awaiting adoption. Truly inspiring.

Dr. Greg Mertz, most appreciative of your turtle expertise and kindness. I love the Odd Pet Vet and the New England Wildlife Center!

And to the educators and librarians out there, my deepest admiration and gratitude. Because of you, the books I write find the readers who need them most. Thank you for caring about, understanding, seeing, and knowing all the students who come into your classrooms and libraries every day.

Finally, to my readers. You are my heroes. Every day you show up. Every day you dig deep and find the courage to be you. Stay true to you. You are special.

With so much gratitude,

Elly

PS It truly takes a village. Thank you all!

Smart Cookie

Finding Perfect

Give and Take

Always Be You,

Elly

EllySwartz.com